By the same author

A Person Shouldn't Die Like That

You're Never Too Old to Die

You're Never Too Old to Die

Arthur D. Goldstein

Random House: New York

Library of Congress Cataloging in Publication Data
Goldstein, Arthur D
You're never too old to die.
I. Title.
PZ4.G6413Yo [PS3557.0388] 813'.5'4 74-9093
ISBN 0-394-49431-8

Manufactured in the United States of America
9 8 7 6 5 4 3 2
First Edition

You're Never Too Old to Die

Guttman stood with his feet apart, hands clasped behind his back, the stub of a cigar clenched between his teeth. It was hot in the sun, but he wouldn't take the one step backward to be in the shade of the portico. One step back would be one step closer to Mrs. Kaplan.

"It would hurt you so much, you should have a little soup?" Mrs. Kaplan asked.

"Mrs. Kaplan, in the first place, I ate so much at lunch, I'd be sick from another bite. In the second place, with the cold I'm getting, I couldn't taste the soup, anyway, to tell if it's good or bad. And in the third . . ."

"I'm not asking you to take a bite, just a swallow. And it wouldn't hurt your cold, a little chicken soup."

"A bite, a swallow. Thank you, but I really don't . . ."

"All right," Dora Kaplan said, sighing deeply. "I wouldn't say another word. Just because I made the soup special . . . So what if I shlepped it here in a Thermos, if Guttman don't want soup . . ."

"He don't," Guttman said. "Believe me, I appreciate," he added, a little sorry that he'd been so stubborn. After all, how much would it hurt to drink a Thermos cup of soup? "Maybe the next time you make the soup, if it isn't too much trouble, you could bring it in . . ."

"I'll save some," Mrs. Kaplan said. "It'll keep even to

Monday. By then your cold should be better. Those cigars don't do you no good, you know," she added.

It wasn't a clear-cut victory, Guttman knew. At best, it was a holding action. Sooner or later he would have to taste Dora Kaplan's chicken soup.

"Anyway," Mrs. Kaplan went on, "that isn't the important thing."

Guttman sighed inwardly and tried to concentrate on the game that was being played across the lawn, in the shade of the overhanging oak trees. He wasn't sure of the name, but he was fairly well convinced that it wouldn't do as a spectator sport. Croquet, he thought. Four people, two men and two women, taking turns leaning over and hitting a wooden ball with what looked like short wooden sledge hammers, trying to knock the ball under the little wire hoops. How do you keep score with such a game? Guttman wondered. Maybe there's somebody Italian here. Maybe we could talk them into making a place to play bocce. All these years watching, maybe I'd get a chance to play, he thought.

"I don't know why you won't do it, Mr. Guttman," Dora Kaplan was saying. The "Mr." alerted him. When she'd wanted him to drink the soup, it had just been "Guttman."

"The poor woman, she's had such a shock, and all it would take from you is to talk to her for five minutes. What's so hard about that?"

"Mrs. Kaplan, it isn't what's so hard for me. The question is, why should it be me in the first place?" Then, before Mrs. Kaplan could answer, he continued, "I never met the woman, I never even met the man, either. So how am I supposed to—"

"You met him," Dora Kaplan said. "Two weeks ago they were together, and I pointed them out to you."

"I don't remember."

"I pointed them out. You and Mishkin were playing cards, and I distinctly remember pointing them out to you. They were such a lovely couple," she added with a small sigh of regret.

"Okay, so I forget. But pointing out isn't the same as meeting."

"Details," Mrs. Kaplan responded.

4

"I don't know why you want I should talk to her, anyway," Guttman said.

"Stop being so modest. I read about New York. Your Lois showed my Phyllis the story in the newspaper. So you don't have to be so modest."

"I'm not being modest," Guttman said, remembering what had led to the story that had impressed Mrs. Kaplan. Six months ago, already. A different world, practically. I wonder whether time goes faster now, at my age, or if it was more quick before, when I was young, Guttman thought.

"You solved that murder all by yourself. Otherwise that man would have gotten away with killing those two people."

"He was a sick person," Guttman said. "And he wouldn't've gotten away from anybody. The truth is, the only reason he didn't kill three people, and me the third one, is the police was figuring it out even better than me. I didn't even know who it was, actually."

"You're just being modest," Dora Kaplan said.

Her mind was made up, and Guttman decided not to argue. He couldn't win. And besides, how many people have their names in the newspaper for anything except when they die?

"All I'm asking is you should talk to her," Mrs. Kaplan said. "You wouldn't have to do anything else, not until you decide to take the case."

"Take the case?"

"She's waiting, already, in the library, you should go in and talk to her a minute. It'll make her feel so much better, what's the harm? It would be a *mitzvah*, Guttman."

"Take the case?" Guttman repeated.

"We can talk about that later," Dora Kaplan said, getting up and putting her knitting on the metal table beside her.

She was a small woman, perhaps an inch over five feet, but she hadn't grown too heavy, as so many women do when they reach their fifties. In Dora Kaplan's case, Guttman was sure that the sixties had been reached, too. And not too recently. She stood near the French doors, waiting for him, and with a deep sigh, Guttman followed. He towered over her. Even with the compacting of age, he was a good six feet tall.

5

"Is he going to do it?" Agnes O'Rourke was stationed just inside the main lounge. Guttman was surprised that she hadn't heard every word.

"I told you," Dora Kaplan said. "I'll go make sure Miss Walters is all right."

"It's such a fine thing you're doing," Mrs. O'Rourke said, watching Mrs. Kaplan march off. "Dora's such a kind person, always worrying about everyone else, never a thought for herself."

"Uh huh," Guttman grunted, wishing that she would worry less about him.

"And it'll be so exciting for us to actually have a case to work on. We read all the mysteries, you know."

"Oh," Guttman said.

"We can talk about that later," Mrs. O'Rourke said. "First we should be talking to our client, right, Mr. Guttman?"

"The client, that's this lady Mrs. Kaplan was talking about?"

"They're waiting in the library," Mrs. O'Rourke told him, urging him on with a gentle tug at his elbow.

Unlike Mrs. Kaplan, Mrs. O'Rourke had added formidable bulk with her years. When she urged, it was difficult to resist. Guttman followed reluctantly, pausing only to leave the cigar stub in an otherwise clean ashtray. Am I really doing this? he wondered.

The library was off the hallway leading to the administrative offices and the clinic. It was a small room, with a couch, two easy chairs and a small table with two straight-backed chairs off to one side. There was a chessboard on the table. The large windows looked out over the portico and the lawn beyond, but now the windows were hidden behind heavy drapes, leaving the room dark and shadowed. Only one of the lamps was on. The walls were lined with books, most of them old, the residue of attic cleanings: children's books that had been outgrown, novels that had been popular twenty or thirty years ago, a few textbooks. After all, if you just wanted to sit and read, you could stay at home—you don't have to join the Golden Valley Senior Citizens' Center for that, Guttman thought. And if you happened to live here, it was better to read in your own room. That way, if you put the book down, no one came along to pick it up before you were through. The good books, Guttman had been told, were traded among the residents and rarely found their way to the library.

In the center of the couch, sitting stiffly on the edge of the cushion, was a small, frail woman. Her gray hair was pulled back into an untidy bun, and her pale, almost translucent skin was deeply creased. There were dark shadows beneath her eyes. She sat with her hands in her lap, fingering a crumpled handkerchief. In spite of himself, Guttman found himself comparing the woman to Dora Kaplan. They were about the same age, which made the contrast even more disturbing. Dora Kaplan's gray hair was blued, and it was carefully brushed and probably full of hair spray. Her clothes were always brightly colored, and they fit her better. She sometimes wore sandals, rather than the plain black shoes that were almost a uniform at Golden Valley. Even the glasses she wore to knit or read were colorful, with sequins in the frames. Not that Guttman liked them, particularly, but at least they were . . . lively.

"This is Mr. Guttman, dear," Mrs. Kaplan said gently. "He's going to help you."

Miss Walters didn't look at her. Her eyes seemed focused somewhere beyond her shoe tips.

"Florence, you should talk to Mr. Guttman. He can help you," Dora Kaplan told the woman. She looked up at Guttman. "She's upset."

"Maybe I should talk to her alone," Guttman suggested.

Mrs. Kaplan started to protest, then looked at Miss Walters and shrugged. "Well, I don't know . . ."

"She's not saying anything," Mrs. O'Rourke pointed out.

"We'll wait right outside," Mrs. Kaplan decided. "You can call if you need us." She turned again to the small woman, as if waiting to be told to stay, then sighed and marched out of the room, Mrs. O'Rourke in her wake.

They closed the door behind them, but Guttman could picture the two women assuming positions on either side of the door, as if to prevent entry by unauthorized people. Guttman looked at the woman on the couch for a moment, then wondered what to say. "Miss Walters," he began finally, "I wouldn't want to butt into somebody else's business. I mean, it was Mrs. Kaplan said I should talk to you. It's not like you asked." Guttman thought he saw a flicker in her eyes, but he wasn't sure.

It isn't just how she looks, he thought. It's how she is in her mind. She doesn't go to any trouble with herself. When somebody goes to the trouble, like Mrs. Kaplan, at least you know . . . You know what? That they at least want to look okay, Guttman thought. They want to look young. More important, they don't want to feel old. And that's more important, even than how they look.

"I was very sorry to hear about . . . about what happened," he said. When she didn't respond, Guttman debated between leaving and sitting down. He chose one of the easy chairs, and leaned forward to her. Now that he was seated, he felt better. Before he'd been towering over the woman, like he was going to yell at her, or something. "I don't know what it is that's a problem," he said. "Mrs. Kaplan didn't explain very much. But I don't know, if there's something that I could do to help . . ."

"He didn't die," Miss Walters said in a soft, clear voice.

Guttman's attention had wandered, and he was startled to see her staring at him. "He didn't die?"

"Mr. Cohen. They killed Samuel. He didn't just die. He was murdered."

"Who killed him?"

"He did," Miss Walters said, her voice trailing off.

"Miss Walters, I'm afraid . . ." She looked at him sharply, and Guttman somehow knew that she was waiting for him to tell her that she didn't know what she was talking about. And knowing that, he couldn't say what he was thinking. "I'm afraid I don't really understand too clear," he said. "Maybe you could explain."

"I can't tell you more than that. But he killed Samuel."

"How do you know?"

"Mr. Cohen told me."

"He told you that . . ."

"He knew things," she said. "And he murdered him because of it." Her tone was matter-of-fact.

"Do you have an idea who it is?" Guttman asked.

"Oh, yes."

"Did you go to the police?" She didn't seem to hear him. "Miss Walters, did you go to the police about this?"

"They didn't believe, either."

"What did you tell them?"

"They didn't believe me. They think I'm just an old woman. They think I don't know what I'm talking about."

Guttman nodded sympathetically. He could understand the police's attitude. "Maybe, if you got an idea, you could explain it to me," Guttman said. "If you know who . . . who killed Mr. Cohen, maybe I could help," he added, not knowing why he had asked.

"I can't," she answered, her voice very soft again. "I tried, but no one listens. But he knows . . ."

Her eyes focused on the floor again, and Guttman realized that only her head had moved, just a bit, since he had come into the room. She hadn't even unclasped her hands. "Miss Walters, I don't know if I could do nothing, but . . ." He wished that he could light a cigar, but it wouldn't be right, under the circumstances.

Miss Walters looked at him again, her eyes on his face, studying him. "Help me," she said softly. "He killed Samuel." She turned her head away. "We were going to be married," she said, so softly that Guttman almost didn't hear her. And then she said nothing.

Guttman waited for a moment, racking his brain. "Do you have, I mean, is there anything you could tell me at all?" The woman was sitting rigidly, her eyes hardly blinking. Guttman sighed and stood up.

Mrs. Kaplan and Mrs. O'Rourke were standing on either side of the door. As he stepped out they both looked at him expectantly, and Guttman wondered whether they had been listening at the keyhole. No, he decided. By themselves, either one might. But Mrs. O'Rourke wouldn't without first asking Mrs. Kaplan, and Mrs. Kaplan wouldn't with Mrs. O'Rourke watching.

"Maybe you should take her to her room," Guttman suggested.

"Are you taking the case?" Mrs. O'Rourke asked.

"There's no case to take," Guttman told her.

He waited while the two women went inside, and then walked slowly back to the veranda. What he wanted now was to be alone. What he didn't want was to discuss with Mrs. Kaplan and Mrs. O'Rourke whether he should, as they put it, take the case. What he also wanted was to understand why he had gotten involved in this thing in the first place, even the little bit that he had agreed to. But first he had to find a place to sit and think. The main lounge was out. That was the first place they'd go, after they got rid of Miss Walters. And after that to the snack lounge, where Mishkin would be sitting, waiting for him to resume their pinochle game. Guttman lit a fresh cigar, puffed at it for a moment, staring vacantly across the green lawn to the trees that hid the private cottages on the far side, and then turned and went back inside. It was a nice day outside, but the last place the women would look for him was back in the library.

With the door closed behind him, Guttman felt that he could be reasonably sure of having at least a little time to himself. He stood and looked at the chessboard for a moment, wondering why the game hadn't been finished, and then saw that two moves for white would bring checkmate. It took him a while to figure it out, though. There were quite a few pieces left on the board, and Guttman had to go through a number of possibilities in his mind before he was sure. Someone had set a good trap. After a moment he sat down and began putting the pieces back to their starting position. Slowly he started to play against himself.

"That's an interesting position." Guttman turned his head quickly. He hadn't heard anyone come in. "I'm sorry if I startled you," she said.

"No, it's okay. I was just concentrating."

"You're Mr. Guttman, aren't you?" He nodded. "I thought so. I'm Margaret Brady."

"How do you do?" Guttman said. He tried to remember whether he had seen her before. There were a lot of people at the Center, and Guttman, having made his small circle of acquaintances, starting with Mrs. Kaplan, thanks to her daughter and his, hadn't progressed too far, yet.

Margaret Brady was tall and slim, dressed casually in a denim skirt and a white blouse. Her sharp features and short-cropped gray hair made her look a bit stern at first, but, Guttman thought, she had a good smile. He guessed that she couldn't be very far past sixty.

"It's nice to meet you, Miss Brady," he said, glancing at her hand. There was no ring.

"Call me Margaret, or Maggie. Everyone around here called me Miss Brady for so long, now that I'm retired, I'd rather not hear it. Makes me think I should go back to work."

"You been here a long time?"

"Twenty-five years," she answered.

"Twenty-five years," Guttman repeated. "You'll forgive me, but you don't look . . ."

"I worked here," Margaret Brady said, smiling. "I was head nurse, until I retired a couple of months ago."

"Oh, I see."

"Uh huh. I gather you play chess."

"Just a little bit," Guttman answered.

"Would you like a game? It's funny. I used to think about how great it would be not to have to run around the halls working all day, since this was such a nice place. And now that I don't have to, I keep looking for something to do."

"Everybody has that when they retire," Guttman said. "With me it was the same. One day I stopped getting on the subway every morning and just stayed home. For a couple of weeks I enjoyed. Then all of a sudden I got up one morning and I didn't know what to do. Still, it wasn't so bad then. I'd go shopping with my Sarah, and we could watch the television together. But . . ."

"How about a game?" Miss Brady asked.

"You want white or black?"

"Stay where you are, and I'll take the black." She sat down and took a pack of cigarettes from her skirt pocket, putting it alongside the board, like a poker player might with his money, and began rearranging the pieces.

It took only a few moves for Guttman to realize that she was better than he was, and only by playing over his head was Guttman able to keep the game close. He felt uncomfortable, taking so much time to decide on each move while the woman hardly seemed to think about it at all.

"Another one?" she asked after the inevitable checkmate.

"Okay," Guttman said, looking at his watch. Even if he lost again, as he was sure he would, he'd be able to learn something. And it could help when I play Joseph, he thought. In the second game Guttman spent much more of his time trying to figure out what she was doing and a little less devising his own strategy. If he had been just a little more careful, he thought, he would have won.

"Have you been playing for very long?" the woman asked at the end of the second game.

"Well, I learned the moves years ago, but I only played a little since then. There was a man in the shop who taught me, and sometimes we played on lunchtimes. But lately I don't play too much."

"You've got a good feel for the game," Miss Brady said. "You ought to meet Mr. Carstairs. He's really a fine player."

"Better than you?"

"Much."

"But you play good," Guttman said.

"I'm improving. Ever since I retired I keep looking for things to do." She looked at her watch. "There's time for another game before you have to leave."

"Okay," Guttman said, although he really wasn't too anxious to play any longer. He didn't like to lose even when he was learning. Still, it's better than going out and arguing with Mrs. Kaplan about the "case," he thought. Oy, such a thing to get myself into. Even if he couldn't help feeling sorry for Miss Walters.

"You worked here twenty-five years?" Guttman asked, studying the board.

"Uh huh. But it didn't seem like that long, until toward the end. You know, when I knew I'd have to retire."

"You had to?" Guttman asked. "I'm sorry, but you don't look so old that you'd have to retire."

"Thank you," Margaret Brady said, smiling. "I'll take that as a compliment. I'm sixty-four, and I guess I could have gone on working a couple of years longer. But when Frank left, well, nothing against Dr. Morton, but it just wouldn't have been the same."

"Frank?"

"Frank Aiken. Dr. Aiken. Someone may have mentioned him. We went back together a long ways. Longer than I care to remember, sometimes. World War II. Frank took this place over back in forty-seven, put most of his own money into it, got some extra capital, and really made something out of it. You should have seen this place when I first came out here. Lord . . ." She shook her head at the memory. "Anyway, Frank sold out when he decided to retire. Now there's a board of trustees running the place."

"Dr. Morton doesn't own it?"

"He's just the director. Oh, there may be something in his contract about profit-sharing, but mostly an insurance company and a bank own the place."

"And you didn't feel like working here with Dr. Morton?"

"Well, you know . . ." She puffed on a cigarette and smiled a bit sadly. "Frank and I had worked together so long, it wasn't like having a boss. I'm Godmother to his youngest. Anyway, with Dr. Morton, I guess it would have been like starting out all over again, and I was close enough to retirement that I just decided it was as good a time as any." She stopped suddenly. "I'm talking too much."

"Why? Two people sit down and talk, how can they talk too much?" Guttman asked.

"Because we're supposed to be playing chess."

"Okay, so we'll play chess." Guttman moved a pawn in what his grandson Joseph had called a "gambit." Unfortunately,

Miss Margaret Brady seemed to know exactly how to handle it, and Guttman quickly found himself in a position he didn't like. It was time to concentrate hard.

"Ahah! So this is where you been hiding."

Guttman didn't have to look to know it was Dora Kaplan. Even if he hadn't known her voice, who else was looking for him? "I'm not hiding. I'm playing chess," he said, turning his head.

"Agnes and I look all over for you, and you say you're playing chess. That's some kind of consideration, Guttman."

"How's Miss Walters?" Guttman asked.

"She's resting, the poor dear. I'm sure she feels better now you're going to help her."

"She told you I said that?" Guttman asked.

"What else should we have told the dear woman?" Agnes O'Rourke asked, stepping a little further into the room.

Guttman couldn't think of an answer. For a moment they were silent: Mrs. Kaplan and Mrs. O'Rourke waiting for him to respond, and Miss Brady leaning back in her chair, smoking a cigarette and looking slightly amused and a bit curious.

"I'll talk with you later," Guttman said finally. He hadn't made up his mind yet whether he was going to allow himself to be pressured into actually doing anything, but he knew he wasn't going to fight that battle now, not with Miss Brady sitting across the table from him.

"Less than an hour and it's time to go home," Mrs. Kaplan pointed out.

"So I'll come out before then. First there's a game to finish."

Mrs. Kaplan looked at the chessboard, but unable to judge how long the game might take, she finally shrugged her shoulders. "We'll be waiting in the snack lounge," she said. Then she left, Agnes O'Rourke right behind her.

"She's mad at you," Miss Brady said.

"That should be the biggest problem I got in my life," Guttman said. And when he thought about it, he realized that it probably was, at the moment.

"What's it all about? If you don't mind my asking."

"I don't mind." Guttman relit his cigar. "Mrs. Kaplan, who's

14

a nice lady, got this idea that I'm supposed to help this other lady I never met before, who's got a problem—"

"Miss Walters?"

"That's the one."

"Severe depression. Maybe even a little paranoid," Miss Brady said clinically. "She may be able to work her way out of it, though."

"I hope she feels better, too," Guttman said.

"What is it you're supposed to do to help her?"

"I wish I knew," Guttman said. "It's about her boyfriend who died."

"Cohen."

"That's the name."

"He had a heart attack, didn't he?"

"I don't know. I mean, I think that's what somebody said."

"Well, what . . . I mean, how are you supposed to help?" Miss Brady asked.

"Like I said, I ain't sure. The thing is, this Miss Walters got an idea maybe something wasn't right. Maybe somebody done something to this Cohen."

"I heard about that, of course. She's been talking of nothing else since Cohen died. What is it she suspects?"

"She didn't say, exactly."

"Well, how are you supposed to help?" Clearly, Miss Brady was at a loss.

"It's because of something that happened in New York, before I came here. There was a person who was killed, and I knew him. So Mrs. Kaplan got this idea . . ." Guttman found it difficult to explain the rest of it.

"Wait a minute, of course. You're the one!" Miss Brady said. "I heard about it, probably from Mrs. Kaplan, but I didn't pay too much attention. You solved a murder, right?"

"I didn't really solve anything," he told her. "I asked some people some questions, and things came out different from what I figured. I almost got killed from it," he added.

"That sounds exciting," Margaret Brady said. "Lordy, I haven't had any real excitement like that since the war."

For a moment Guttman thought she was making fun of him.

"Well, maybe in a way it was. But now Mrs. Kaplan thinks I'm Dick Tracy or somebody. A case, she calls this. There's a sick lady with crazy ideas, and Mrs. Kaplan wants I should make a big deal." He sounded harsher than he felt, and he was sorry about his choice of words. "The thing is, what could I do? Besides, who's to say what happened in the first place?"

"So Miss Walters thinks someone murdered Mr. Cohen," she said quietly.

"She says 'he killed him.' "

"Who?"

"She don't say who. She only says 'he.' " Guttman looked at the chessboard. "It's your move or mine?"

"Yours. I moved my knight last. What are you going to do?"

"About Miss Walters, I don't know. About the game, I'm gonna lose, like the other ones."

"I don't know. It's far from over. But it wouldn't be a bad idea if you studied some openings."

"To be honest, I tried. My grandson Joseph, he's got books on chess, and I looked at one. Only it's hard to concentrate."

"Well, maybe Mr. Carstairs could show you."

"So maybe I'll ask him, sometime," Guttman said, wondering whether he ever would. Fifteen minutes later he had lost the game.

They were waiting at the usual table. Mrs. Kaplan busy with her knitting, while Agnes O'Rourke browsed through a movie magazine and Mishkin played solitaire. It was Mishkin who noticed him first.

"Nu, Guttman? Did you forget we was supposed to finish a pinochle game?"

"Who could forget?" Guttman asked, sitting down. "Only I didn't get the chance, until now. So now we can finish." Guttman wasn't anxious to play cards—especially after losing three games of chess—but it would help in dealing with the ladies until it was time to go.

Dora Kaplan waited until the hand had been dealt before she spoke. "Well, Mr. Guttman?"

"Well what?"

"Don't be obtuse," Mrs. Kaplan said.

Guttman made a note to look the word up when he got home. Mrs. Kaplan liked to use big words. She had a book for her vocabulary, which she studied. "What do you want I should say?" Guttman asked.

"Say whatever you like, but play a card. Spades is trump," Mishkin told him, leaning forward to straighten the cards on the table. Mishkin had a little trouble managing that, with his girth. Obediently, Guttman led a card. "Are you going to help?" Mishkin asked.

"I don't know what I could do," Guttman said. "I mean, I feel sorry for her and everything, but what should I do?"

"Surely there's more to it than that," Mrs. O'Rourke said. "What else?"

"She's practically accused someone of murder," Mrs. O'Rourke answered. "That's not a thing to be taken lightly."

"I'm not taking light, but the thing is, in the first place, all she says is 'he.' And in the second place, the doctors say this Cohen just died, right?"

"Heart attack," Mishkin said. "I meld kings," he added, putting the cards on the table. "And the marriage in trumps."

Guttman glanced at his hand. Well, at least it isn't for enough money to matter, he thought. If he got clobbered, he'd owe a dime. The only reason they played for money was that Mishkin said it was the only way he could enjoy the game.

"And that's it?" Mrs. Kaplan asked mildly.

Guttman waited for the attack. "What else is there?" he asked again. "She went to the police and told them, didn't she? And they said to her there was nothing wrong. So what do you want me to do?"

"The police can make mistakes," Mrs. Kaplan said. "And who knows what she actually told them, the poor woman."

"Mr. Guttman, would you like a cup of tea?" Mrs. O'Rourke asked, deciding to try kindness.

"Thank you, but no."

"Mishkin?"

"It would be very nice, but I'm not allowed."

"Maybe a cookie, then?"

"That would be nice, too," Mishkin said. "But I'm not allowed that, either."

"Oh, Mr. Mishkin, surely one cookie wouldn't hurt you," Agnes O'Rourke said.

"Believe me, it isn't my idea."

"They're diet cookies," Mrs. Kaplan said.

"It isn't the weight I'm worried about. The doctors got me on a strict diet. Anything that tastes good, I'm not allowed."

"Well, it wouldn't hurt you to lose a couple pounds," Mrs. Kaplan said.

"Why?" Mishkin demanded, leaning back in his chair and patting his stomach. "At my age I'm supposed to be skinny like a movie star? When I was young I was skinny." He paused. "You don't believe me? So don't."

"What's wrong, you can't eat a cookie?" Mrs. Kaplan inquired.

"What's wrong? How should I know. Forty years I'm a plumber. So now a doctor talks to me, it isn't even in English. In Latin you expect me to understand what a doctor says is wrong with me?"

"Age doesn't mean you can't be attractive," Mrs. O'Rourke said. "Cary Grant is nearly seventy, and he's certainly attractive. And look at Mr. Guttman. You don't see him getting fat, do you?"

Guttman was embarrassed, and at the same time he couldn't help feeling flattered at being compared to Cary Grant. Even if it was only because he wasn't fat. "I walk a lot," he said. "In New York, I always took long walks. Fast, like Harry Truman used to."

"That's very interesting, I'm sure," Dora Kaplan said, bringing him back to reality. "But it still doesn't answer the important question, Mr. Guttman."

"Okay, so you got an idea what I should do?"

"Well, as a matter of fact, I thought about it. While you were playing your chess with that . . . nurse."

A nurse, Guttman suspected, was something like a servant maybe. "Okay, so tell me."

"Firstly, we should find out what the police know. Then we could decide what really happened. After all, nobody's saying we should launch a full-scale investigation until we know more than now," Mrs. Kaplan declared.

Full-scale investigation? Guttman sighed. "Okay," he said reluctantly. "So let me make a suggestion now. Let me make the suggestion that everybody thinks about this tonight. There's lots of questions, and we could talk about it tomorrow. Something like this, you don't just go jumping into. Now it's almost time to go, anyway," he added quickly, looking at his watch.

Mrs. Kaplan opened her mouth, then closed it. She could

wait another day. Guttman waited, then turned his attention to the cards, which for the first time were coming his way. He might be able to salvage something from the afternoon.

At five o'clock he joined the other "commuters" standing in front of the building. Inside, the residents had begun returning to their rooms to prepare for the evening. After dinner they would sit where they had during the day, or else watch television. Some of them had TV sets in their rooms, but most chose to watch in one of the three alcoves off the main lounge, so they could have company . . . those who could get around by themselves, of course. The others remained in their rooms, or were wheeled out to join the main group. Three alcoves, three color TV sets, the gift of a grateful child relieved at being able to dispose of a parent without too much guilt, each set permanently tuned to a different network. It was easier to ask the viewers to get up and move than to decide what show should be watched. When Mishkin had explained it, Guttman thought it made sense. And sometimes, usually on Friday, there were movies. Other nights there were lectures, and once in a while, outings to ball games or shows. And once a month, on a Saturday night, there was a big dance. Guttman had succeeded in avoiding the last one.

Despite all of this, most of the residents envied the commuters. They were going home to their families, for them it wasn't like being put away. For them it was like . . . day camp. A happy way of spending their daylight hours, a way to enjoy their retirement without being "removed." Guttman, perhaps more than the others, appreciated his situation. After all, he'd been there only a short time, and before that, he'd spent three years alone.

Lois was late. When she arrived, Guttman was alone in the driveway, patiently smoking his cigar and only a little worried that something might have happened. He threw the cigar away before getting into the car. Lois didn't like to see him smoking too much, and she complained that it bothered her when she kept the windows closed and the air conditioning on.

"Hi, Pop," she said, leaning across the front seat to kiss him on the cheek. "I'm sorry I'm late, but I got tied up in a meeting, and then when I stopped at the supermarket it was mobbed, and as usual I got on the slowest line. Honestly, I thought the check-out girl was catatonic."

"So where am I going in such a hurry?" Guttman asked, wondering exactly what "catatonic" meant. Lois often used words he didn't understand, but he rarely mentioned it.

"How'd your day go?"

"Okay," he answered, wondering whether he should tell her about it or not.

"Just okay?"

"It's plenty, a day is okay," Guttman told her.

"Don't you like it there, Pop?" Lois asked suddenly. "I've been thinking about it, and I wonder whether I pushed you into it, you know, so if you don't want to keep on going, I mean . . ."

"I like it," Guttman said firmly. "I admit, when I first went, I wasn't so sure, but I figured I'd try. And then with that arts-and-crafts lady . . ."

"I thought you'd enjoy working with your hands."

"I should make an ashtray, or a belt from pieces of leather? Never mind. The thing is, yes, I enjoy there. There's some nice people, and today I played some chess. Maybe I'll get good enough to play Joseph."

"Are you sure, Pop?"

"I'm positive." Guttman smiled at her concern. She was so worried that he wouldn't be happy there. Well, he thought, it's partly my fault. For so long I kept saying I didn't want to come here to California, I wanted to stay in New York, it's natural she should be worried I'm not happy. And it had been strange, at first. Lois didn't even look the same to him. Since she and Michael had moved West, he'd somehow kept remembering her younger and younger, although he'd seen her when she came East to visit. Now, looking at his daughter, Guttman saw that she was approaching middle age. Me, I look in the mirror every day, I don't see so much change. But her, I look and she's older, so how come I don't feel older? But she don't look old. She got a good figure, like her mother, and she dresses casual in slacks and looks good, and she gets lots of exercise, always running around and playing tennis on Saturdays and Sundays. Guttman realized that he felt very proud of his daughter. Even if she did worry too much.

"Something funny happened today," he said as they stopped for a traffic light.

"Oh?" Lois asked suspiciously.

"It's your friend Mrs. Kaplan."

"How are you two getting along?"

"What's not to get along about?" Guttman asked. "But what happened today . . ."

"And what was that?"

"The light changed," he prompted. As she maneuvered the car into another lane, he thought of the words he wanted. "There's this old lady there, at the Center, a Miss Walters. She ain't so well, and she was going to marry this fellow, someone I never met, named Cohen, only he died."

"That's sad," Lois said.

"It's sad when anybody dies," he agreed. "But I think maybe it upset her thinking a little, this Miss Walters. Now she's going around saying how Cohen didn't just die, how somebody killed him."

"It isn't true, is it?"

"The doctors was there," Guttman said. "It's like a hospital there, with doctors around and nurses all night long, they tell me."

"Of course."

"So anyway, now Mrs. Kaplan has this idea about being a detective and finding out about the whole thing."

"I wouldn't call that being a detective," Lois said. "I'd call that being a *yente*."

"So we agree on that," Guttman said. "But the thing is, she wants I should do something about it."

"Like what?"

"Like I should be a detective, too. And it's your fault," he added.

"Me? What did I do?"

"The newspaper story. I shouldn't've sent you that clipping."

"I don't understand, Pop."

"Mrs. Kaplan saw the story, no? Your friend Mrs. Kaplan."

"Now wait a minute. She's not my friend. Her daughter Phyllis is."

"Whatever, she saw the story in the newspaper, and now she wants me to make like a detective on television. Only she's going to help, too." Guttman screwed up his face in dismay, and was a little surprised to see his daughter laugh.

"Oh, Pop . . ."

"What's so funny?"

"I'm sorry," she said, still laughing. "But it's funny."

"I'm glad you think so."

"It's just that I can't picture you as a detective, that's all."

"So that makes two of us. Now if only we could get Mrs. Kaplan to make it three," Guttman said, smiling back at his daughter.

Guttman took a sip of his coffee, found it to have cooled to the right temperature, and sat back to light an after-dinner cigar. Since Michael smoked a pipe, there was no problem with the cigars, except that Lois kept taking away their ashtrays to clean them and forgetting to bring them back. She was trying to get Michael to give up smoking altogether, and if she succeeded, Guttman knew he'd have a battle on his hands.

"Mom, can we watch part of the game tonight?" Joseph asked.

Guttman's oldest grandchild was twelve, and didn't seem as young as a twelve-year-old should. But now kids get older when they're younger, he thought.

"I don't know. I may want to watch something," his mother said.

"But it's better in color," Joseph explained.

"Did you finish your homework?" Lois asked.

"Most of it."

"Go finish the rest of it, and make sure your brother does his, too."

"Then can we watch the game in the living room?"

"We'll see, then," Lois said.

Joseph waited for a moment, then brushed his hair back from his eyes, sighed, and went off to the bedroom he shared with his brother David.

"You want another piece of cake, Pop?" Lois asked.

"How about me?" Michael demanded.

"You're on a diet."

"A diet?" Michael repeated. "I haven't gained a pound in three years—ever since I lost that extra weight. What kind of a diet am I on?"

"I don't want you to gain them back, either," Lois said. "I like you the way you are. Pop?"

"Not for me," Guttman said. "I ate too much already."

"Take it," Michael said. "Then when she isn't looking, I'll finish it."

"Never mind," Lois said. "Pop, you hardly ate anything at all. I don't know how I'm going to fatten you up."

"I been like this all my life," Guttman told her, knowing that she was really teasing. "You want I should get fat now?" For a brief moment he remembered Mrs. O'Rourke's remark about Cary Grant, but he wasn't going to mention it. Lois wouldn't have understood—or perhaps she would have understood too well.

"Okay," Lois said. "Listen, while I get the baby ready for bed, why don't you tell Michael about what you told me in the car?"

"There's nothing to tell, really," Guttman began.

"Pop's girl friend, Mrs. Kaplan—"

"She ain't my girl friend!"

"That's Phyllis Sobel's mother, isn't it?" Michael asked.

"Right. Anyway, she got all excited about that business in New York, and now it seems there's a bit of a mystery at the Center, and she wants Pop to play detective."

"What kind of mystery?" Michael asked his father-in-law.

"Oh, it's really kind of touching," Lois answered for him. "This old couple were planning on getting married, and then he died, and now the poor woman's lost touch with reality. Pop says she claims someone killed her fiancé."

"That is sad," Michael said.

"Well, that's not the part I thought was funny," Lois said. "I meant the part about Pop being a detective."

"I think he'd make a good detective," Michael said.

"Oh, come on now . . ." The baby cried, and Lois was reminded of her chores.

"Are you going to do anything about it?" Michael asked when she had left the room.

"What should I do?" Guttman asked. "The lady's sick. This Cohen person just died. They got doctors at the Center and everything. The thing is, when you get old, sometimes you don't like to think about dying. Especially, I guess, if you're going to get married. A thing like that must be hard, anyway."

Michael nodded and finished his coffee. "I'd better make sure the kids are doing their homework. It's a shame about the old lady." He stood up, thought for a moment, then said, "You know, I'm not an expert on this sort of thing, but it seems to me that the big thing about being a detective is just knowing how to think. You know, the stuff on television is all nonsense, anyway."

Guttman smiled and shrugged. Then he sat and wondered why he felt disturbed, as he did. It just didn't make sense, but there was something. He wondered about it until David came in to tell him that the game was about to start. The boys, and their father, were avid Dodger fans. With Zayde rooting for the Mets, they became even more so. Throughout the game Guttman tried to concentrate, tried either to forget or to understand what was bothering him. Even a Met victory didn't make him feel much better. Finally, before he went to sleep, he decided what he would do, and that helped a little.

Guttman stood on the corner and watched as Lois made her turn and drove off. Then he walked away from the Golden Valley Senior Citizens' Center and crossed the street to a phone booth. He dialed the number he'd copied from the phone book while the family had been eating breakfast, and listened to it ring three times.

"San Martin Police Department, Sergeant Porter speaking."

"Yes, I wonder, could you tell me how to get to the police station?"

"Pardon?"

"I want to come to the police station, only I don't know how to get there," Guttman explained.

"Do you want to report a crime?"

"I want to talk to someone there, only first I got to get there."

"Where are you now?" the policeman asked. Guttman told him the names of the intersecting streets. "Okay, just drive down Central for about a mile, then . . ."

"I'm not driving a car," Guttman said.

"Look, if you want to report a crime, we can send a car to pick you up . . ."

"It wouldn't be necessary, but thank you. Maybe a bus goes by?"

"Sure," the voice said. "But if you like . . ."

"It's nothing so special you have to send a car," Guttman

said, hoping that they weren't going to trace the call and come and get him anyway. The last thing he wanted was to be seen getting into a police car. "The bus is fine," he said, "if there's one that goes near the station."

"The number ten bus stops right on the corner. Tell the driver you want to get out at Fulton and Sutter. Then walk one block east."

"Thank you very much," Guttman said, hanging up quickly. He wondered whether the policeman thought he was—what was the word—a crank?

The police station surprised him a little. It was a two-story building with a lawn in front, and it looked more like what Guttman thought a courthouse, or even a Red Cross building or something like that, should look like than a police station.

He climbed the wide steps and pushed open one of the double doors. The air conditioning was set high, and he felt a chill. But the interior looked more like what he expected. There was a big desk, like a judge's bench, behind which sat a uniformed policeman. There was a bench against the opposite wall, and a bulletin board with an assortment of papers pinned to it. The walls were a dirty green. This was what police stations looked like in all the movies.

"Can I help you?" He was black, which surprised Guttman, because the nameplate on the desk said "Sergeant Porter," and the man he had spoken to on the telephone hadn't sounded black.

"Thank you," Guttman said, moving closer to the desk. "My name is Guttman. I think I talked to you on the phone a while ago."

"Oh, yeah. You wanted directions. I guess you got here all right."

"They was very good."

"You wanted to talk to someone, but you didn't say who," Sergeant Porter told him.

"You remembered?"

"I wrote it down. Standard procedure for all calls."

"That's very good," Guttman said. "Yes, I would like to talk to somebody, only I don't know who."

"Well, maybe if you'll tell me what it's about, I can help."

"Well, the thing is . . ." He was finding it difficult. "There was a person named Cohen, died maybe a week or a week and a half ago, and a lady, Miss Walters, said she talked to a policeman about it. So that's who I want to talk with, also."

"Walters . . . Oh, yeah," Sergeant Porter said, looking just a bit less friendly. "She's the old lady with the bug about . . ."

"That's the one," Guttman confirmed.

"Look, Mr. . . ."

"Guttman. Max Guttman. With two t's," he added as the policeman wrote it down.

"Thanks. Mr. Guttman, I don't know what that old lady's been saying, but believe me, she's, well . . ."

"I know," Guttman said. "But still, could I talk to whoever it was . . . ?"

The policeman looked at him for a moment, then shrugged and picked up the telephone. When he spoke, Guttman couldn't hear what he said. "Lieutenant Weiss will be with you in a couple of minutes," Sergeant Porter said after a moment.

"Thank you very much." Guttman wandered over to the bulletin board and gazed idly at the notices. A schedule of hours, something about a picnic, and tickets for baseball games. Weiss. So, he thought, it could be Jewish. And it also could be something else. So it makes a difference? A police lieutenant yet.

"Mr. Guttman?" He hadn't heard him approaching. "I'm Lieutenant Weiss. Can I help you?"

The man looked to be in his mid-thirties, not very tall and almost skinny, with some of his hair already gone. Lieutenant Weiss was wearing a striped shirt with a tie, and gray pants with a blue sport jacket. Guttman didn't think he looked very much like a police detective.

"I'm Max Guttman. How do you do?" They shook hands. "I'm sorry to bother you like this."

"That's okay. What can I do for you?" the detective asked pleasantly.

"Could we talk a little. I mean, maybe you got a couple of minutes?"

"Sure. We can use one of the interrogation rooms. Then we

won't have to walk upstairs." He led the way back through a swinging door and down a corridor, then held open another door for Guttman. The room was practically bare. Two windows were protected by bars, and in the center of the room, under a bank of fluorescent lights, was a long table and three hard wooden chairs.

"Please, sit down," Weiss said, closing the door behind him. Guttman took one of the chairs, while the detective stood with his back to the windows and crossed his arms. "Now, what can I do for you?"

"I don't mean to be a bother," Guttman said uncomfortably. "The thing is, this Miss Walters—at the Golden Valley Center— she's all upset. It's about this Mr. Cohen, what died not so long ago. Maybe you remember."

"I remember," Weiss said.

"Well, Miss Walters is all upset, and I figured, maybe if I talked to you, I could say something to make her feel better."

"She still thinks someone killed her boyfriend?"

"She told you about it?"

"Oh, yeah," Weiss said with a sigh. "She kept calling, too. I went out and talked to her, but it didn't seem to do much good."

"That was very nice of you," Guttman said.

"My grandmother's seventy-five," Weiss said, "and sometimes she gets some strange ideas, too. I figured it would make her feel better. Besides, you've got to check up on all of these things. Ninety-nine percent are cranks, but you can't be sure unless you check them all out."

"And?"

"And I told her just what I'll tell you, Mr. Guttman. Cohen had a heart condition. He'd had it for years. We talked to his former doctor, and he confirmed it. Cohen was seventy years old and he died of a heart attack."

"That's positive?"

"The nurse found him while he was still alive. They got the oxygen in, doctors all over the place. Are you a resident there, Mr. Guttman?"

"No. I only belong during the day."

"Well, anyway, I'm sure you know that they have the same

medical facilities as a hospital," Weiss said. Then, after a moment, he asked, "Do you live alone?"

"With my daughter and her husband," Guttman said. "Only . . ."

"Yes?"

"Only I'd appreciate if you didn't call her, or anything. She'd make a big fuss, and the only reason I came is because this woman is all upset, so maybe if . . . maybe I could convince her there's nothing wrong, she'll feel better. That's why I don't want to be a bother . . ."

"If you don't believe her, why did you bother coming at all?" Weiss asked. "Why not just tell her there's nothing to it, and let it go at that?"

"She says nobody listens to her," Guttman said. "So now, at least, I can be honest and say I talked to the police. I don't want to lie to her."

"Well . . ." Lieutenant Weiss smiled a bit. "I guess I can understand that."

"I guess there's nothing else to say," Guttman said after a moment.

"If you really want to help her," Weiss said, "you should get her to stop talking like this. As long as she goes around thinking someone killed her boyfriend, well, she's going to have trouble, shall we say, adjusting to it?"

"It's hard for her," Guttman agreed. "I'll do what I can." He stood up, then thought of something. "I wouldn't want you should think I came here because I didn't think the police done their job, or nothing. It's just that, when she talks like that, some of the other people at the Center get upset, too. They got nothing else to think about, you know, so . . . Well, now I could tell everybody that things is normal, and nobody was fooling around."

"That's fine, Mr. Guttman. You do that," Weiss said, and Guttman felt very sorry that he'd bothered to try to explain.

"I'm sorry to take so much of your time," he said, moving toward the door.

"If it makes you—or anyone else out there—feel better, it's worth it," Weiss said. He walked to the front door with

Guttman, told him where he could get the bus, and then they shook hands. "You know," the detective said, "you did the right thing by coming here. Now you just tell everyone not to worry, okay?"

"Thank you," Guttman said, again.

Walking to the bus stop, he tried to decide whether Detective Weiss, a lieutenant of the police, was a nice person or not. He was polite, but at the same time he was almost too polite. Like with a baby, very patient. Nu, so you're an old person, Guttman. And old persons get funny ideas sometimes. How sharp do you think? As good as when you were young?

The ladies were waiting for him. They were sitting in the main lounge, where they could watch the front door, and they spotted him as soon as he came in. Mrs. O'Rourke started to get up, but Mrs. Kaplan didn't move, and her friend sat back. Guttman wished that they hadn't been there, but he knew he had to talk to them.

"Nu, Guttman?" Mrs. Kaplan asked. "I thought maybe you weren't coming today."

"I came."

"Did you think about things? They had to give Miss Walters sleeping pills last night, she was so upset."

Guttman sat down facing them and leaned forward, hands clasped between his knees. "I went to talk to the police this morning."

"Then you're going to work on the case?" Mrs. O'Rourke asked expectantly.

"There's no case, like you call it, to work on."

"But—"

"Miss Walters says this police lieutenant didn't listen. She's wrong. I talked to him. Did you know Cohen had heart trouble before? This wasn't the first time." Their silence told him that they hadn't known.

"The police made an investigation, they talked to his old doctor. Cohen just died from a heart attack."

"They investigated thoroughly?" Mrs. Kaplan asked.

"They made an investigation," Guttman answered.

"The poor woman. You . . . it was her last hope."

"She's still sleeping from the medicine?" Guttman asked.

"Uh huh."

"So when she gets up, I'll try maybe to talk to her. But she shouldn't go around saying somebody murdered Cohen. Even with her mind the way it is, that isn't right." Guttman got up and walked away from the women. Maybe he'd find Mishkin and play some pinochle. It would take his mind off things. He wasn't ready for chess this morning.

Just after lunch, as Guttman was preparing to go outside to sit in the shade and enjoy a cigar, one of the nurses came up to the table.

"Mr. Guttman?" she asked.

"That's me."

"Dr. Morton would like to see you."

"Me?"

"In his office. I'll show you the way." She was young, and, Guttman thought, like many of the others on the staff, she wasn't too polite.

"Do you know what it's about?" he asked.

"Dr. Morton didn't say," the girl answered.

Guttman shrugged and stood up. He didn't like the idea of being summoned to the director's office, but there was nothing to do but follow the girl. He couldn't very well tell the nurse to find out what Dr. Morton wanted, then come back to tell him. He had taken a physical examination when he joined the Center, but that was about two months ago, and it wouldn't take this long to find something wrong, he decided. So it must be something else.

Dr. Morton got up from his desk as the nurse ushered Guttman into the office. He was of medium height, several inches shorter than Guttman and a bit overweight. Not exactly fat, Guttman thought, but he should go on a diet. The doctor's hair was gray and thinning, but he wore it fairly long and had a fashionable mustache.

"Mr. Guttman, it's nice to meet you," Dr. Morton said, extending his hand. "I'm sorry we didn't get to chat when you first joined our family. I like to try to meet all of the new members, but there never seems to be enough time."

"It's nice to meet you, too," Guttman said.

"Well, how are you getting along?"

"I'm okay."

"I notice that you dropped out of the arts-and-crafts program," the doctor said, consulting a folder on his desk. He made it sound as if Guttman had done something wrong. "Arts-and-crafts programs are really quite worthwhile," the doctor continued. "It's important that we have something to occupy ourselves. Have to maintain some interests, keep active mentally. And physically, too. Have you tried croquet?"

"I watched a little bit," Guttman said.

"You should try it. Or shuffleboard. Exercise, in moderation, is very important as we advance in years."

"I agree with you," Guttman said. "As a matter of fact, I was wondering, maybe it would be a good idea to have a bocce court."

"Bocce?"

"It's an Italian game, kind of like bowling without the pins."

"But you're Jewish, aren't you?"

"Lots of Jewish people eat pizzas, don't they?" Guttman asked, a little annoyed.

"Of course," Dr. Morton said, smiling. "You just surprised me, that's all. Do you play bocce?"

"I used to watch, back in New York, and I thought it would be an interesting game to play."

"Well, we'll have to look into it. Meanwhile, you might want to see whether you could join in a croquet match."

"I might."

"There are other activities, too," Dr. Morton went on. "We have an excursion scheduled for next week, as a matter of fact. I'm sure you've seen the notice on the bulletin board. A trip to the Los Angeles Art Museum."

"I don't think I noticed," Guttman lied. Mrs. Kaplan had already mentioned it.

"Well, if that doesn't appeal to you," Dr. Morton said, "I can tell you about the next event we have. It isn't quite firmed up yet, but we're planning on having everyone attend a Dodger game in a few weeks. Are you a baseball fan, Mr. Guttman?"

"I like to watch," Guttman admitted, wondering whether the only reason he had been called to the office was because he hadn't talked to Dr. Morton when he first joined the Center.

"Tell me, how are you getting along with the other members here?" Dr. Morton asked, taking a pipe from the rack on his desk.

"Okay."

"Well, that's fine, Mr. Guttman. That's fine." He seemed to lose himself in thought. "I, uh, I understand you spoke to Miss Walters."

"Yesterday." So here it is, Guttman thought. "Mrs. Kaplan asked me to talk to her."

"Mrs. Kaplan. Ah, yes. She likes to, well, keep track of things, doesn't she?"

In spite of himself, Guttman smiled. He was surprised, though, that Dr. Morton knew so much of what was going on. After all, he and Mrs. Kaplan weren't regular residents.

"And after you spoke to Miss Walters, you went to the police, didn't you, Mr. Guttman?"

"They called you," Guttman said, finally understanding.

"A matter of courtesy. But that's why I wanted to talk to you. Lieutenant Weiss told me about your attitude, that you seemed to understand the situation with Miss Walters . . ."

"I know she's upset," Guttman said. "That's why I went to the police in the first place. I figured that way I could tell her honest what was going on, and maybe she'd feel better."

"Of course," Dr. Morton said. "I gather she's still claiming that someone killed Mr. Cohen."

"Uh huh."

"Did she say who?"

"No," Guttman answered, shaking his head.

"I was hoping perhaps she'd said more. If we had something

specific, we might be able to talk her out of it. But as it is . . ."
Dr. Morton shook his head, and then sat back in his chair. "You
know," he said, "the problem isn't just that she called the police.
I wish it were that simple. Unfortunately, she made some other
calls as well. Mr. Cohen's family, a nephew, and a former
business associate, I think, and she even seems suspicious of us
here, too. That's to be expected, though."

"I didn't realize she was bothering so many people,"
Guttman said.

"When we finally found out about the calls, we had the
phone in her room disconnected. It was the only way to keep her
from bothering these people. Mr. Cohen's nephew seemed
particularly upset. Said his wife was distraught."

Guttman didn't know what that meant exactly, but he had a
general idea. "I didn't realize," he said lamely, feeling foolish for
having added to Dr. Morton's problem.

"Well, you certainly haven't done anything wrong," the
doctor said. "Although it might have been better if you'd
stopped in to see me first."

"I didn't think about it," Guttman admitted.

"No harm done. But the question is, what do we do now?"

"I don't know. I been thinking about it myself, all morning,"
Guttman said.

"I'm sure you have. It must be very awkward for you. If I
may make a suggestion?"

"I'd appreciate it."

"I think it would be best for Miss Walters if you tell her
exactly what happened. I don't know whether she'll believe you,
but she may." The doctor sighed. "She's practically obsessed by
this idea of hers, and unless she shows some signs of getting
over it, I'm going to ask Dr. Friedemann to talk to her."

"Dr. Friedemann?"

"He's a psychiatrist. One of the best, I might add. He does
some consultant work with us from time to time. There are
emotional, as well as physical, problems connected with aging,
you realize."

"Naturally. There's emotional problems with everything in
life," Guttman said.

"Miss Walters should be awake now. I think it would be better if she stayed in her room, though. Would you mind seeing her there?"

"Now?"

"Unless you'd rather not."

"No. Now is as good as any time, I guess."

It was Guttman's first trip upstairs, and he was disturbed that it seemed more like a hospital than he'd imagined. There was the faint odor of antiseptic, and a nurse's desk near the elevator opposite the large stairway.

"This is our medical wing," Dr. Morton said, as if reading Guttman's thoughts. "Some of our patients are confined to their rooms. Those who can function on their own are in the regular dormitory wing, which allows us to provide more supervision for those who aren't."

"The ones who'd be stuck alone, doesn't that make them feel worse—being here, I mean?"

"That's one theory. Of course, we have to consider the effect they have on the residents who are healthy. Seeing someone who isn't well can be an unpleasant reminder of things they'd rather not think about."

"I guess it's hard, either way," Guttman said.

"Yes, it is."

They had stopped in front of one of the rooms. Dr. Morton knocked on the door, and a middle-aged nurse opened it. "Is she awake?" Dr. Morton asked.

"Yes, but she's just lying there. I tried to get her to eat something, but she just picked at the food. If she doesn't perk up by this evening, I think you may want to start her on intravenous," the nurse said.

"Well, keep me informed. This is Mr. Guttman. I'd like him to talk to Miss Walters, but I think it would be best if you stayed in the room."

"Are you going?" Guttman asked.

"Yes. As I mentioned, Miss Walters seems, well, somewhat paranoid. I think she blames me, among others, for Mr. Cohen's death. She gets upset when she sees me."

"That's too bad."

"But not unusual. As director here, as well as a physician, she probably feels that I could have done something to save Mr. Cohen. There's a tendency among paranoids to view everyone in authority as a threat."

"I guess so," Guttman said, not quite sure that he understood.

"Mr. Guttman, I don't know whether this will help Miss Walters, but I want you to know that I appreciate your cooperation."

"I'll do what I can," Guttman said.

He stepped inside the room cautiously, and the nurse closed the door behind them. Miss Walters was lying on her back, her gray hair spreading across the pillow. She was staring at the ceiling, her hands clasped across her chest.

"Someone to see you, dear," the nurse said. "Mr. Guttman is here." Miss Walters didn't move, and the nurse looked at Guttman and shrugged.

"Miss Walters, it's Max Guttman," he said, taking a step closer to the bed. "Remember, I talked with you yesterday. Miss Walters?"

Slowly, almost painfully, the woman turned her head to look at him.

"It's about what we talked about yesterday," Guttman said. "What you told me. I want you should know, I went to the police today. I talked to them about what you said."

Miss Walters only blinked.

"I found out from them that Mr. Cohen had heart troubles for a couple of years," Guttman said. "Maybe he didn't tell you about it," he suggested.

The woman didn't move.

"Miss Walters, believe me, I'm sorry. But all I could do was find out what the doctors already told you. The police investigated, and it was just a heart attack. It's very sad that it happened, but that's all it was. Nobody done nothing to Mr. Cohen."

The woman turned her head a bit more, staring hard at his face, and then nodded slightly and closed her eyes for a moment.

Then she turned and stared up at the ceiling. After a moment Guttman left.

He spent the rest of the afternoon playing pinochle, losing hand after hand to Mishkin and trying to ignore the studied coolness of both Mrs. Kaplan and Mrs. O'Rourke. He was very happy when it was finally time to go outside and wait for Lois.

Guttman enjoyed the weekend. Friday evening, in the Little League game, Joseph played shortstop for three innings and made only one error, which didn't lead to a run by the opposition. And, at bat, he also managed to walk twice. Even though his team lost, it was a personal triumph, and the entire family shared it with him.

Saturday, while Lois did some shopping and Michael went out to play golf, Guttman watched over his granddaughter, young Sara, and that evening, when Lois and Michael went to a dinner party, he and Joseph played chess while David alternately watched his brother beat Zayde and watched television. On Sunday the family went to the camping area nearby for a picnic. By the time he went to bed that night, Guttman was very tired. And he'd hardly thought about Miss Walters at all.

Monday morning was different. The sun was shining warmly, and as he crossed the street to the Center, Guttman remembered that today was the day for the trip to the museum. Mrs. Kaplan wouldn't be around all day to pester him. He might even try to play some croquet this morning, if he could find someone to tell him the rules and show him how. He thought about going straight to the library, to see whether Miss Brady was there and whether she wanted to play chess, but decided instead that he would like another cup of coffee first. So everybody makes mistakes, he thought later. At least, I could have enjoyed feeling good a while longer.

40

They were waiting for him. The three of them watched him approach, Mrs. Kaplan without her knitting, Mrs. O'Rourke with her movie magazine lying closed on the table, and Mishkin hardly looking interested in his game of solitaire.

"Good morning," Guttman said. "Did you have a nice weekend?"

"Miss Walters died," Dora Kaplan said.

"Oy," Guttman whispered. "When did it happen?"

"Yesterday morning," Mishkin said. "They found her in the morning."

"What . . . what was the cause?"

"The cause? Who knows?" Mrs. Kaplan said. "They said she just gave up. A severe depression."

Guttman sat down wearily and shook his head.

"Mr. Guttman, would you like a glass of water?" Mrs. O'Rourke asked solicitously. "Are you all right?"

"I'm all right, thank you. It's just a shock, that's all." How, he wondered, could you feel so bad about a person you hardly even know? Why not? A person is a person.

The four of them sat at the table most of the morning, talking very little. Guttman played cards with Mishkin, but neither of them was really interested in the game. It was something to do. In the same way, Mrs. Kaplan picked up her knitting and Mrs. O'Rourke browsed through her magazine. But she didn't read any of the interesting parts to them. And Mrs. Kaplan paid no attention at all when it was announced that the bus was leaving for the museum.

After an equally somber lunch Guttman went to stand outside, in the back, to smoke his cigar. It was really more comfortable inside, where the air conditioning was set at the same level all the time, but he felt confined there. Okay, so it bothers me still, he thought. So why shouldn't it? Better ask why it should. It's not like you really knew the woman. She was practically a complete stranger. Nu, so what is it, Guttman? You're thinking maybe she was right? All of a sudden you got a whole big thing in your head she was right, and now somebody killed her, too? You been watching television too much, Guttman. You got too much sense for that. Besides, even if it was true, that's not what's really bothering you, he told himself. So, if not that, then what? If I knew, he told himself, I'd tell me. Oy, when you start thinking like that, it's better you shouldn't think. Next thing you'll be talking out loud to yourself. After a while he went inside again, turning toward the library. It would be better to be gone for a while.

He hesitated at the door, then decided to go in. There was no place else to go, really. Margaret Brady was playing chess with someone. He was neatly dressed, wearing a dark suit, a white shirt and a tie. His gray hair was combed back flat, and his thick glasses gave the man's thin face an owlish look. Unconsciously Guttman patted down his own unruly hair. A full head of hair, at seventy-two. Gray, but lots of it. Miss Brady smiled at him and he tried to smile back, but neither she nor her opponent spoke.

Guttman didn't really watch the game closely. They seemed to be so intent that he felt he would be intruding, although he kept one eye on the game. So far as he could tell, it looked pretty even. But Miss Brady's expression said she was losing, and eventually she did.

"Hi," she said to Guttman. "Mr. Carstairs, this is Mr. Guttman. I told you about him."

"How do you do?" Mr. Carstairs said.

"Nice to meet you," Guttman answered.

"Miss Brady tells me you play."

"Not so good as she plays," Guttman said honestly.

"Mr. Carstairs taught me everything I know," Miss Brady said.

"Hardly," Mr. Carstairs said, with a small smile. "But you do learn quickly."

"Would you like to play?" Miss Brady asked Guttman.

"I'd lose, for sure," he answered quickly, thinking that Mr. Carstairs didn't look too anxious for a new opponent. "I think what I should do is take some lessons."

"Then play a game with him," Miss Brady said, getting up from the table. "He can't resist telling you when you make a bad move. It's a good way to learn."

Reluctantly, Guttman sat down and finished arranging the pieces. On his third move Mr. Carstairs made a suggestion, and showed Guttman what could happen in another three or four moves if he persisted with his original idea. Two moves later there was another suggestion. By the time they reached what Joseph called the middle game, Mr. Carstairs stopped making suggestions, and Guttman realized that from here on in, the game would be played to win. The expert Mr. Carstairs accomplished that rather quickly.

"You have a good feel for the game, Mr. Guttman," Carstairs said, standing up.

"That's what I told him," Miss Brady agreed.

"You should work on the fundamentals a bit more, though."

"Thank you," Guttman said.

"Well, I must be going. Thank you for the game," Mr. Carstairs said.

"It was my pleasure," Guttman replied.

"He's a little stiff, but nice," Miss Brady said when Carstairs had left. "And he's a fanatic about the game. You should have seen him during the Fisher-Spassky match. Watching on TV, following every move, keeping track, mumbling to himself, playing it out on a pocket board."

"It's a hard game to really learn good," Guttman said.

"If you like, I can lend you a couple of books. It might help."

"I don't know if it would do any good, but I guess it wouldn't hurt."

"Fine. I'll get them from my cottage and give them to you before you leave."

"You live in one of the cottages?" Guttman asked. There were four that he had seen, across the back lawn and partially hidden by a stand of trees.

"Lived there practically since I first came here," Miss Brady said. "Not much, but I call it home. Living room, bedroom, kitchen. It's enough for one person."

"I'm sure it's very nice," Guttman said.

"Well, you can come visit, if you like. Pick the books up, take those you think you can use."

"I . . . That would be very nice."

"Fine. Come on, then, might as well get them now, before we forget. Unless you'd rather play another game."

"No," Guttman said. "To tell you the truth, I don't feel much in the mood to play chess."

"Something wrong?" she asked. Guttman shrugged. "Okay," she said, "then let's go look at the books."

Feeling self-conscious, Guttman followed her through the main lounge and out to the back lawn. He didn't turn his head to see whether Mrs. Kaplan or Mrs. O'Rourke might be watching, but he felt a little better when they reached the trees and were hidden from the main house. The cottage was small, with clapboard sides and a porch running across the front. It looks like a vacation cabin in the mountains, Guttman thought, not like a year-round house. Of course, he reminded himself, here it doesn't get very cold in the winter.

"Here we are," Miss Brady said, holding the door open for him.

Guttman indicated that she should go first, and then followed her. The living room was larger than he'd expected it to be, and much nicer. The walls were all paneled with wood, and the furniture looked to him as if it were a western style. Heavy wooden chairs with deep cushions, brightly colored scatter rugs on the deeply waxed floor, and bookcases lining the wall opposite the entrance. It has everything, he thought, except a fireplace. A counter with two stools separated the kitchen area from the living room.

"It's very nice," Guttman said.

"Thanks. Let's see, where are they . . ." Guttman watched as she moved back and forth in front of the bookcase. "Ah, here they are," Miss Brady said, reaching up to take several books down. "Let's see what we've got here." She brought the books to the coffee table and sat down on the couch. Guttman sat down next to her.

"Well, here's Nimzovitch. Charlie's fond of him, but if you ask me, it's a little too much."

"Charlie?"

"Charlie Carstairs. You can take it if you like, but I'd advise against it."

Guttman looked through the book, the pages packed with

small type and notation after notation of moves and strategies. "I think maybe I'll take your advice about this one," he said.

"Well, this is a good one," Miss Brady said, handing him a book called *Chess Openings*. "It covers less than it should, but what's there is pretty straightforward. This one isn't bad," she said, handing Guttman another book. "And Evans is okay, too," she added, leaving Guttman with three books, two more than he'd expected.

"Can I offer you something? There's some lemonade, if you like," Miss Brady said, returning the other books to the shelves.

"I . . . Yes, that would be very nice," Guttman said, deciding that if Mrs. Kaplan and Mrs. O'Rourke were keeping track of him, it was their problem, and he wasn't going to worry about it. He crossed the room and sat on one of the stools at the dining counter while Miss Brady poured two glasses of lemonade. He tasted his, and told her it was very good.

"Wish I could take credit for it, but all I did was open a can."

"Maybe you could tell me the kind. I could get my daughter to buy some, next time we go to the supermarket."

"Have you lived with your daughter for long?" she asked after showing him a can of the lemonade.

"About three months."

"Like it?"

"Yes, mostly."

"Yes, mostly," she repeated. "A little bit of no, perhaps?"

"So what's perfect?" Guttman asked, smiling. "But it's mostly okay now. At first it was a little strange, and Lois was always making a fuss. Also, there was nothing to do."

"So you joined the Golden Valley Senior Citizens' Center to make friends, right?"

"What's wrong with that?"

"I'm only teasing," Miss Brady said quickly. "Let's face it, I'm here too. When Frank decided to sell his interest in the place, I could have left too. But I own this cottage, and we worked out a deal with the new owners, so here I am. Didn't really have anyplace else to go," she added.

"I'm sorry."

"That's life, Mr. Guttman. Besides, there really isn't anyplace else I feel like going. Maybe I have roots here, I've been around so long. Guess I feel more secure in familiar surroundings."

"That I could understand," Guttman said. "It was hard to decide to come here after living all that time in New York, even when there was nobody there. At least here, you have friends, you have people to be with."

"True," Miss Brady said. "Listen, I . . . well, I don't know, but I was just wondering about what you said before. If there's something bothering you, and you feel like talking . . ."

"It's not such a big thing," Guttman said.

"Well, I realize it's none of my business . . ."

"It ain't that," Guttman said quickly. "It's just about Miss Walters."

"Ah . . ." Miss Brady said. "She went Saturday night."

"I thought it was Sunday morning."

"That's when they found her. She went in her sleep."

"I guess that's the best way," Guttman said.

"I don't know. I've seen a lot of people go. Saw them during the war, when lots of them went hard. I've been a working nurse for forty-two years. At first I used to think it was better to go in your sleep. But some—especially in the war—there was a moment, kind of a look on their faces . . ." She shook her head and lit a cigarette.

"So now maybe you think that's better?" Guttman asked.

"Now I don't think about it," Miss Brady said. "But you're upset about Miss Walters, huh?"

"There's something bothers me about it. When I talked to her, she was all upset about the man she was going to marry, Cohen."

"Uh huh."

"I don't know why it should bother me, but it does. It's something . . ." Guttman shrugged and smiled. "It's funny, you can't think of something, and then as soon as you start to talk out loud, you know what it is."

"And what is it?" she asked.

"The way everybody acted. Everybody was the same. Even me. Everybody acted like Miss Walters didn't know what she was talking about. Even Mrs. Kaplan and Mrs. O'Rourke, all they wanted was to play detective."

"I'm not sure I understand. Do you mean that you think . . . I mean . . . that Miss Walters was right?"

"To be honest, no. But the thing is, if she wasn't an old lady, people would've acted different. But just because she was old, everybody figured she didn't know what she was saying, automatic. Even me," he added.

The former nurse was quiet for a moment, then nodded her head. "I guess I understand," she said, "but what else could you do?"

"Oh, it ain't what I done. If I think about it, maybe I was making a *mitzvah*. You know what that is?"

"I don't think so."

"It's a good deed, like. Something that's supposed to make a blessing for you, with Him. I went to the police station and I talked to the detective there. Then I talked to the doctor, and I saw Miss Walters and told her how there wasn't nothing wrong. I was trying to make her feel better, so you could say it was a *mitzvah*."

"But there's still something sticking in your craw," Miss Brady said.

"It bothers me. Not what I done, or even what I was thinking. But the why. That's the thing."

"But what can you do now?"

"I'm gonna learn a lesson," Guttman said. "I'm gonna remember that I'm not a kid, either. And there's nothing wrong with how I think, just because I'm old. Sometimes I'm right, sometimes I'm wrong. But that was always the same. Never was I always right about everything."

"Who is?" Margaret Brady asked with a smile.

"Maybe I should get back," Guttman said, handing her the empty glass. "I promised to play pinochle. I like chess better, but I promised . . ."

"I hope the books will help. Just don't try to learn too much too fast, otherwise I won't be able to keep up with you."

"I don't think that's gonna happen," Guttman said. "Are you going back?"

"No, I think I'll read for a while."

"Maybe I'll see you tomorrow," Guttman suggested.

"I'll be around. No place else to go," she added, smiling.

Walking back to the main building with the books under his arm, Guttman stopped to watch the croquet game for a moment. Maybe it's got some points, he thought, but I'd rather try playing bocce.

It wasn't until he and Mishkin were playing the second hand of pinochle that Mrs. Kaplan broke her strained silence. She looked pointedly at the books Guttman had brought back with him and nodded her head significantly.

"Nu, Guttman, it's all over?"

"What's all over?"

"You didn't believe Miss Walters, right?"

"I went to the police, didn't I? I talked with them, no?"

"And they said heart attack," Mrs. Kaplan finished for him. "Other things can look like a heart attack, you know."

"How do you know so much?" Mishkin asked.

"I watch television. I read books," Mrs. Kaplan said. "And Miss Walters, she just stopped living, too, is that it?"

"Go ahead," Guttman sighed. "Say it already."

"What's to say?" Mrs. Kaplan asked.

Mrs. O'Rourke put her magazine down and waited.

"If there's nothing to say, what are you asking?"

"You ask me, I'll tell you. Suppose, just suppose . . ."

"I already thought about it," Guttman interrupted.

"And?"

"And what? You got a suggestion?" Guttman put his cards face down on the table. "Mrs. Kaplan, believe me, I thought about it. I saw Miss Walters in her room on Friday, and I told her there was nothing to do. I wished there was something, even something I could say. I wished I could say you're right, somebody killed Cohen and now we're gonna get them. But that only happens on television, in the movies. And maybe in the books you read. But that ain't real life."

Dora Kaplan stared at him for a moment, then, tight-lipped, she picked up her knitting. Guttman wasn't sure that she was convinced, but he picked his cards up, anyway. But he couldn't enjoy the game at all.

"Look," he said after a while, "let's everybody talk about this once and for all. Okay?" The others looked at him, then adjusted themselves into positions of attention. "Now, the first thing is, everybody is upset."

"Of course," Mrs. Kaplan said.

"Okay. Now, the second thing is there is a little wondering, thinking maybe, just maybe, Miss Walters was right. That's the second thing, right?"

"It is possible," Mrs. O'Rourke said softly.

"There are doubts in my mind," Mrs. Kaplan agreed.

"And you?" Guttman asked Mishkin.

"You want an honest answer?"

"No, I want you should lie."

"Okay. So by me, I don't know. I got no reason to think she wasn't just a little crazy, maybe. But just because of that, it don't mean I'm right."

"You don't have to work on the case, then," Mrs. Kaplan told him.

"Wait a minute. Nobody's working on nothing yet," Guttman said quickly.

"I think we have to do something, Mr. Guttman," Agnes O'Rourke said. "Even if there's only the slightest chance, it would be on my conscience if we didn't try."

What is there to try? Guttman thought. Okay, so if you feel that way, just say it and forget the whole thing. I'd like to, he thought. Only I can't. "I tell you what let's do," he said to them. "Let's all think about the whole thing real good, and then—"

"We already thought," Mrs. Kaplan said. "And you said you thought, too."

"So we could think some more. So far, all anyone done is think how bad they feel. That's not the same thing as going and doing something about it. That's a different kind of thinking." He looked at them, and knew that he was right. They really

49

didn't know what they wanted to do. "And another thing," he said. "We shouldn't talk to no one about this."

"How are we to question the suspects if we don't tell anyone about this?" Mrs. O'Rourke asked.

"First you got to get a suspect. Then you worry about questioning," Guttman said.

"All right. We won't talk about it yet," Mrs. Kaplan said.

"That means nobody," Guttman told her. "Nobody here, nobody at home, either."

"I still don't see why it has to be such a secret," Mrs. O'Rourke said.

"Because if people find out, they're gonna make trouble. They're gonna tell us we're crazy, and then nobody's gonna pay attention when we try to find things out."

"And also, Guttman don't want his daughter to find out about what he's doing," Mishkin said.

"Never mind that."

"How should we proceed?" Mrs. Kaplan asked.

"Is everybody agreed it's a secret?" They all nodded—even Mishkin, who rarely seemed to talk to anyone except them. "The next thing is, somebody's got to be in charge," Guttman said hesitantly.

"Naturally," Mrs. Kaplan said. "Why do you think we've been waiting for you to make up your mind?"

"You want me to be in charge?"

"Of course," Mrs. Kaplan told him. "You're the only one who has any experience, after all."

Some experience, Guttman thought. "Okay, but that means everybody got to do what I tell them. And remember, I'm not a hot-shot like you might think. A detective I'm not," Guttman reminded them, knowing that they had already made up their minds that he was.

"What is it you'd have us think about, Mr. Guttman?" Mrs. O'Rourke asked.

"Well, we should first look at what we got to begin with," Guttman said. "And so far, all we got is a maybe. A what if. What if Miss Walters was right."

"If she was right, then someone may have killed her, too, to prevent her from talking," Mrs. O'Rourke suggested.

"And maybe she just died, like they said with Cohen," Mishkin said.

"No, they'd have killed her to keep her from making any more trouble," Mrs. O'Rourke said. "That's the way it always is."

"It don't matter about Miss Walters," Guttman said, shaking his head slowly.

"It doesn't matter?" Mrs. Kaplan asked.

"That's right. It's logic," Guttman explained. "Even if it was how Miss Walters died, to keep her shut up, it don't tell us nothing. First, we couldn't prove it, right?"

"They could do an autopsy," Mrs. O'Rourke said.

"You need proof that something happened, or you got to get somebody in the family to say so," Mrs. Kaplan declared. "And we have neither."

Guttman was grateful for her expertise. If I'm gonna get into something like this, he thought, maybe I should watch more mysteries on television. "The thing is," he said, "if that's what happened, it was because of something what was already done to Mr. Cohen, right?"

"It makes sense," Mishkin agreed.

"So that brings us back to him. We got to see if there's anything to what Miss Walters was saying."

"He had a family," Mrs. O'Rourke said. "Maybe we could get them to ask for an autopsy."

"You still got no suspicious reasons, no proof," Guttman told her, remembering what Mrs. Kaplan had said.

"So what do we do?" Mishkin asked.

"We got to see if we can find out what persons might have had a reason for killing Cohen."

"How does that help?" Mishkin asked.

"If you want to prove something," Guttman explained, "first you got to have somebody to prove it against. If you got a reason, then at least you got a place to start looking."

"Well, what shall we do?" Mrs. O'Rourke asked.

"Well, we got to ask people things, we got to find out all about Cohen. Maybe he had some friends, you mentioned a family . . ."

"But you said we shouldn't talk about this," Mrs. O'Rourke protested.

"You don't have to walk up and say, 'Listen, I'm making like a detective, who do you think killed Cohen?' " Guttman said. "Just talk to people, maybe tell them about what Miss Walters was saying. Make fun on her, if you want, it don't make a difference now. See what they say back to you."

"I'll take care of it," Mrs. Kaplan said. "I know how to handle it."

If anyone knew how to find out about people, Guttman thought, Mrs. Kaplan was the one. "Okay," he said. "So that's the first thing."

"Is there a second thing?" Mrs. O'Rourke asked.

"One thing at a time," Guttman answered.

"We'll start right away, then," she said, getting up from the table.

"We'd better wait until tomorrow," Mrs. Kaplan said. "It'll give us a chance to think about what we want to ask."

"Fine," Guttman said, wondering why Mrs. Kaplan was so helpful all of a sudden.

"Then we'll meet here tomorrow," Mrs. O'Rourke said, as if they hadn't been meeting at the same table every day for six weeks.

"Okay," Mishkin said. "So now can we finish the card game?"

The investigation began before Guttman even arrived at the Golden Valley Senior Citizens' Center the next morning. After all, Agnes O'Rourke and Jacob Mishkin were full-time residents, and Mrs. Kaplan's suggestion to wait notwithstanding, neither of them was inclined to let the opportunity pass. Mrs. Kaplan seemed to have arrived early, herself, so that when Guttman went into the snack lounge, he found their usual table deserted. A short stroll around the grounds showed him that they were hard at work. He thought about joining them, but he really didn't know anyone else well enough to simply walk up and start talking. Except Miss Brady.

He tried the library first, and since it was empty, he sat down for a moment and tried to concentrate. A crazy man in New York had once tried to make him drink a cup of tea with poison in it. It'll look like a heart attack, the man had said. Is that why I'm so much involved? No, but it showed that kind of thing is possible. But that was a crazy man, he reminded himself. So how hard would it be for somebody what wasn't crazy to give this Cohen some poison, and also to Miss Walters? And what kind of a person goes around poisoning people, anyway? It's got to be someone with a big reason. Especially with them, because they were old.

Okay, so if it happened, there must've been a big hurry. That was something to remember. But go back, take a look at what you already thought. Could anybody just go and get this kind of stuff to give to Cohen? That was another question. Not the main thing, but something to think about later. The main thing, he reminded himself, was to find out about Cohen.

Guttman walked across the back lawn slowly, stopping to look at the rack of croquet mallets, even picking one up to heft it. But he kept himself from looking to see whether anyone was watching him. That's another question, he thought. Why should it bother me so much if I go talk to Miss Brady?

She was sitting on the porch of her cottage, in a rocking chair, reading the morning paper. A cup of coffee was on the small table next to her, along with a full ashtray. Miss Brady peered over her glasses as he approached, then let them hang from the string around her neck.

"Well, Mr. Guttman, good morning."

"Good morning. I hope I'm not bothering."

"Not at all. Like a cup of coffee?"

"Thank you."

"It's instant, if that's all right."

"It's fine," Guttman said. "With milk and sugar, please."

It was nice on the porch, cool in the shade of the over-hanging trees, and quiet. Guttman didn't want to sit in her chair, so he leaned back against the porch railing, suddenly thinking how much things change with age. A youngster, he sits on the porch rail. But me, I'm not so sure any more I won't fall, so I just lean. Miss Brady pushed open the screen door and came out with a cup in one hand and a folding chair in the other.

Guttman took the chair from her. "It's very nice here," he said. "I didn't want to disturb you . . ."

"I usually sit here in the mornings. Sometimes right through lunch. Kind of my routine. Breakfast, then drive in to get the papers—I could have them delivered, but I like an excuse to go somewhere—do a little shopping, then I sit here and read the paper. Funny, how when you really don't have anything to do, you get into a strict routine."

Guttman nodded and smiled a little, remembering how he had planned his days when he was alone, and how difficult it was when the weather was bad and he couldn't go out. He sipped his coffee and looked for the right words.

54

"Did you get a chance to go through any of the books?" she asked.

"No. That is, I looked a little, but not really."

"Mr. Carstairs has been talking about organizing a tournament, if he can find enough people."

Guttman nodded. "What I came about is to see maybe I could ask you a couple of questions," he said awkwardly.

"Shoot."

"You remember, we was talking yesterday about Miss Walters?"

"Uh huh. You're still not sure whether you should have believed her or not, are you?" Miss Brady said.

"I'm pretty sure," Guttman answered. "But not positive, no."

"And now you're going to . . . investigate?"

"Well, I wouldn't call it . . . Yes," he admitted. "How did you know?"

"I played bridge with Mishkin last night."

"And he told?"

"Agnes O'Rourke was there. You know, she hardly lets Mishkin out of her sight."

"I didn't know that," Guttman admitted, wondering about it for a moment. "What do you think?" he asked.

"I think it's a good idea."

"You do?"

"Sure. If something's bothering you, why not look into it? If there's nothing in it, then no harm's done. And the big thing is you don't just sit around stewing."

"Do you read mystery books?" Guttman asked, suddenly suspicious.

"I'm addicted to them," Miss Brady said, laughing.

"Mrs. Kaplan and Mrs. O'Rourke, too. That's how this got started in the first place. Mrs. Kaplan coming and telling me she got a case I should work on."

"Well, I guess we're a little like kids, you know, playing make-believe games," Miss Brady said. "But there's always the chance that there is something to it."

"Did you know Miss Walters or Cohen very well?"

"They were both here while I was still on staff, so I got to know them a bit. But we weren't particularly close. You know, a couple of words here or there, once in a while I'd see them at dinner."

"The others, Mrs. Kaplan and Mrs. O'Rourke, even Mishkin, are talking to people to see what they could tell about them."

"Is that what you wanted to ask me?"

"Not exactly. I got some other questions. You see," he said, leaning forward, "if something really happened, then we got to look first for anything to do with Cohen. With Miss Walters, she could've just died from being depressed. But if anything happened, then it was because of Cohen, to keep her from talking."

"That makes sense."

"This Cohen, he had a heart attack, right?" Guttman said. Miss Brady nodded. "So if somebody killed him, is it possible you could make a heart attack happen?"

"Sure," Miss Brady said.

"That I already figured, from something that happened in New York. But what I got to know, now, is how hard is it?"

"Pardon?"

"Well, let's say you give somebody something that makes them have a heart attack. How hard is it to get the stuff?"

"Well, that depends," Miss Brady said slowly. "If you're worried about an autopsy, it can be very hard to get something that may not be detected. But if you just . . ." She nodded her head and lit a cigarette, then studied Guttman for a moment.

"I think I see what you're driving at. Something that wouldn't show up in an autopsy would be hard to manage. But if it just looked like a heart attack, and Cohen had a history of cardiac trouble, then it would be simple."

"Mostly," Guttman said, "I was thinking about how hard it would be to get the stuff, whatever. But it's also possible you could scare a person to death, no? I mean, a person with a bad heart."

"Yes, but that would be risky."

"Because maybe they wouldn't be scared enough, and then they could tell on you, right?"

"Uh huh. There's no way of really knowing just how the

heart will react to stress. You get people with heart conditions going through some very rough situations and showing little or no effect. Then again, they can just topple over, for no apparent reason."

"So if somebody was actually trying to kill Cohen, it wouldn't be too smart if they went out and tried to scare him to death."

"It could have been an accident," Miss Brady said. "Suppose that someone was talking to him, maybe having an argument, and Cohen got upset, then . . ."

"Sure," Guttman said. "And most likely he just had a heart attack by himself."

"True," she agreed. "But you're going to look into it, anyway. So where do we begin?"

"Well, it wouldn't be possible to get an autopsy," Guttman said, "so what we're doing is looking for people what got a reason for killing Cohen. Also, maybe if we could get an idea if it could've been something besides a regular heart attack. You know, like maybe the doctors didn't do such a good job of checking when they found him."

"You mean, they may have simply assumed a heart attack because of his prior history?"

"That's it."

"And that's my job?" Miss Brady asked.

"Well, you was a head nurse, and besides, you're the only one to know what to look for."

"And the only one who might be able to look at the records and talk to the staff without arousing too much suspicion," Miss Brady added. "I assume we're keeping all of this quiet. No point in alerting anyone, just in case."

Guttman nodded in agreement, although he hadn't been as concerned about alerting anyone as he had been that Lois might find out.

"I'll get right on it," Miss Brady said. "When do you want me to report to you?"

"I guess we'll all meet at lunchtime."

"The first full meeting of the Golden Valley Irregulars, huh?"

"I don't know from that . . ."

"Sherlock Holmes had a group called the Baker Street Irregulars," she explained.

"Sherlock Holmes, I ain't."

"But we're sure irregular," Miss Brady said. "See you at lunch."

With everyone else working, Guttman decided that there was nothing for him to do at the moment, and so he found a copy of the morning paper in the lounge and went into the library to read. There was an interesting article about trying to teach porpoises to speak.

Looking at them as he passed through the cafeteria line, Guttman thought that Mrs. Kaplan didn't look any too pleased to have Miss Brady there. She seemed to be trying to pretend that the other woman wasn't sitting next to her. Well, he thought, I'm not gonna worry what Mrs. Kaplan thinks about that.

"Is that all you're having to eat, Mr. Guttman? A bowl of soup?" Mrs. O'Rourke greeted him as he reached the table.

"It's vegetable soup. Vitamins inside," Guttman said. "Also, there's crackers, and I don't like a big lunch, anyway." He sat down and broke the crackers into the soup. "So," he said, "everybody's here." Mrs. Kaplan gave Miss Brady a sideways glance. "Miss Brady's helping," Guttman continued. "She used to be the head nurse here, so she can find out things."

"That's very good," Mishkin said before putting a large forkful of cottage cheese in his mouth. "Low-calorie cheese, even," he said. "No fat. It tastes like paper."

"There are some interesting aspects to the case developing," Mrs. Kaplan said.

"Maybe we should wait till we finish eating," Guttman suggested.

"What difference?" Mishkin asked.

"You can concentrate better when you're not chewing," Guttman told him.

"Maybe you concentrate better. Me, I finish eating and I start going to sleep."

"I think Mr. Guttman is right," Mrs. Kaplan said, looking not at Mishkin but at Miss Brady.

Oy, Guttman thought. This I need? Still, lunch was finished in relative silence, and a bit more quickly than usual. They decided to sit outside afterward, where they were less likely to be overheard. Miss Brady offered the use of her cabin, and Mishkin, thinking about a comfortable chair, thought it was a good idea, but after a look at Mrs. Kaplan, Guttman said no. "We don't want to make it look too much like it's a secret goings-on," he explained.

"Big secret," Mishkin said. "You think we're the only ones with the same idea?"

"What do you mean?"

"I mean what I said. Everybody you talk to, they was wondering the same thing as us."

"Except for those who are sure that Miss Walters was touched," Mrs. O'Rourke added.

"I think we should proceed with the reports," Mrs. Kaplan interrupted. "Now, I spoke to . . ."

"Mrs. Kaplan, if you don't mind, I think we should listen to Miss Brady first," Guttman said. Clearly, Mrs. Kaplan did mind, so Guttman explained. "You got to remember," he said, "the first thing we got to know is was it possible that somebody could've killed Cohen and the doctors wouldn't've known. Otherwise, everything else don't mean anything."

Reluctantly, Mrs. Kaplan agreed. "As you wish," she said.

"Well, the first thing I did was check Cohen's medical file," Miss Brady began immediately. "I remembered offhand that he had had some heart problems a while back, but I figured it would be a good idea to check it out anyhow. That part's legitimate. But I got a chance to talk to Joan Wideman, too. She's a good kid, and she was on duty the night that Cohen died. I broke her in when she first came here, fresh out of school, so we get along pretty well. Anyway, from what Joan says . . ."

Miss Brady paused for breath, and the others held theirs. "From what she says, they just did a superficial examination. The signs were there—chest pains, labored breathing. Cohen didn't last very long, though. They tried the usual emergency stuff, but it didn't help. And from what Joan says, I'd have to say that it could have been induced and no one would have spotted it with the kind of quick diagnosis they did."

Miss Brady waited, and the others nodded their heads, pursed their lips, and looked a bit relieved. They had cleared the first hurdle. It was possible. "Now, as for the second part," Miss Brady went on. "I went through a couple of my books, and there are several drugs that could have caused the symptoms that Cohen showed, particularly in a case where a previous heart condition existed."

"Would it be hard to get these drugs you mention?" Guttman asked.

"Not the easiest thing in the world, but not impossible. It would take a little planning for most people, but that's all. The right combinations of fairly simple things would do it."

"What did you mean when you said for most people?" Mrs. O'Rourke asked.

"Well, around here, for example, it wouldn't be hard at all. These drugs aren't particularly dangerous, and the security on them isn't the same as for, say, narcotics. Inventory isn't as strict, either, so anyone around here who knew what to look for would have been able to get the stuff pretty easily."

"How many people would know what to look for?" Mrs. Kaplan asked.

"Hard to say. But if you decided to commit a murder and wanted to cover it up, I guess you'd just make it your business to know what to look for. All you'd have to do is go to the library and look it up, really."

"That's a good point," Mishkin said. "I wouldn't have thought of it."

"Okay," Guttman said after a moment. "So now we got number one, it's possible. So now we can go to number two."

"What's that?" Mishkin asked.

"Number two is people what might have had a reason."

"Finally," Mishkin said. "I was talking to—"

"It's Mrs. Kaplan's turn," Guttman interrupted.

"Thank you," Mrs. Kaplan said. "First, to support what Mr.

Guttman has suggested earlier, Miss Walters had no family whatsoever. And everyone seems to have been fond of her, so if anything did happen to her, it seems likely that it had to be because of her relationship to Mr. Cohen."

"We already knew that," Mishkin said.

"Go ahead, Mrs. Kaplan," Guttman told her, hoping to avoid an incident.

"Thank you," she said. "Now, as for phase two of our investigation, I think we should start by looking close to home."

"Close to home," Mrs. O'Rourke repeated softly.

"Close how?" Guttman asked.

"Close enough," Mrs. Kaplan answered, with a quick look at Miss Brady. "Did you know that there was quite a . . . well—how shall I put it?—practically a battle over Miss Walters' affections? It seems we had quite a romantic triangle, right here at the Center."

"A triangle," Agnes O'Rourke whispered. This might turn out to be as exciting as her movie magazines. True, there wasn't a real Cary Grant around, but still . . .

"Wait a minute," Mishkin said. "I'm remembering something."

"It's hard to believe," Guttman said. Why is it hard to believe? he asked himself as soon as the words were out of his mouth.

"Carstairs!" Mishkin declared.

"Carstairs?"

"Mr. Carstairs," Mishkin repeated.

"Precisely," Mrs. Kaplan said quickly, regaining the floor. "I've learned that he and Miss Walters knew one another before moving here, and their . . . friendship, continued. Until our Mr. Cohen arrived on the scene."

"Oh . . ." Agnes O'Rourke sighed. "And to think I knew them all, and I never had a clue."

"When Mr. Cohen arrived," Dora Kaplan continued, "he began paying quite a bit of attention to Miss Walters. So much so, in fact, that Mr. Carstairs challenged him one day. They had a big fight."

"A jealous lover," Mrs. O'Rourke said.

Guttman glanced at Margaret Brady, but she was looking straight ahead. "You know this for sure?" he asked.

"I remember," Mishkin said. "I wasn't here, but I remember everybody talking about it. It must've been maybe a year ago already. But in a place like this, people remember."

"Lots of people here have arguments," Miss Brady said.

"Sure," Mishkin agreed. "Me, I fight with lots of people. But two men fighting over a woman, that don't happen so often. Not here, anyway."

"Mrs. Kaplan, you said we got to start close to home. This is what you meant?" Guttman asked.

"I don't think it's any secret that Miss Brady is good friends with this Carstairs person," Dora Kaplan replied.

"That might be putting it a bit strongly," Margaret Brady said, with a small smile. "But we're friendly."

"There's a question from all this?" Guttman asked.

"Only that I know that I would be impartial in my judging if Agnes here was a suspect," Mrs. Kaplan said.

"A suspect of what?" Agnes O'Rourke asked, startled.

"Just an example," Mrs. Kaplan said soothingly.

"Because somebody had an argument, that don't make him a murderer," Guttman said. "Not that it isn't important," he added quickly. "It's the kind of facts we got to get, here at the beginning. But if you look on it another way, it's a good thing Miss Brady is friends with Carstairs. I know him, too. It might be easier to talk to him, because of it."

"I see," Mrs. Kaplan said.

"I don't know what you see, but what you give us here is the first person to talk to. If he knew her from before, maybe Carstairs can tell us something about Miss Walters we don't know. It's a place to start, anyway. But you got to figure, in a place like this, practically everybody's gonna be friendly with somebody."

There was a moment of silence, and finally Agnes O'Rourke spoke. "I think Mr. Guttman's right. After all, I've been here five years, and I know just about everyone. It's like a family."

"Who's going to talk to Carstairs?" Mrs. Kaplan asked.

"I'll talk to him," Guttman said.

"You're going to question him alone?"

"You think better a committee?" Mishkin asked.

"I'll talk to him alone," Guttman said. "The rest of you should go ahead talking to other people, asking if there's anything else we could learn."

"Well, I guess we'd better get back to our snooping, then," Miss Brady said after a moment. "I tell you, for a while, anyway, everyone's going to think we're the friendliest bunch of people in the place. Or the nosiest."

"Nosey," Mishkin said. "That I could guarantee."

After a moment they dispersed, and Guttman went inside, thinking that he might find Mr. Carstairs in the library, where he'd first met him. There was no one there, so he sat down and lit a fresh cigar.

There's still something I'm not exactly saying to myself, he thought. In New York, maybe I'd go by the candy store and have a soda and talk with Bensky for a while, and I might get an idea. But Bensky I knew thirty years. Here is nice people, but I only know them a couple of weeks. Okay, he said to himself, so that's enough being homesick for Bensky's candy store. Now figure out what it is on your mind. Sit and think.

That's it, he realized. What else is there to do except sit and think? You play a little cards, maybe some chess, you could learn to play the croquet and maybe one day they'll fix it up for bocce. So what else is there to do when you're old? Just relax and enjoy life, everybody says. You're supposed to. Only it don't work. In this world, if you don't do nothing, then that's what you are. Nothing. Especially if you're old. You got nothing to do, and you're going to make like a detective. And it bothers you, you keep thinking somebody's gonna say you're just a snoop, a *yente* with nothing else to do. A busybody. Also, he thought, it bothers you that you're afraid somebody's gonna laugh.

So laugh, he decided. But what if, just what if, somebody killed Cohen and Miss Walters? Then who's gonna find out if you don't do your snooping? Is anybody else worrying about it? You could apologize for getting into somebody else's business, but you couldn't apologize for letting somebody kill a person and not doing anything about it. A person's got responsibilities, Guttman decided. And just being a little worried about Lois getting mad isn't enough excuse for not doing what you got to do. So maybe somebody is gonna say Guttman's crazy. So let them. But a person's got to do what he thinks is important, old or not.

After a while, feeling restless, Guttman got up to stretch his legs. He strolled out to the back, watched the afternoon croquet game for a moment, and decided that simply walking across the lawn and back for exercise wouldn't appeal to him. But there was no place else to go at Golden Valley. So I got to stay here? he asked himself. He turned around and marched quickly across the main lounge to the front door and outside. Now which way? It didn't matter, but as he reached the street Guttman turned left.

Golden Valley had been a private home once, an estate with a large main house, several outbuildings and expansive grounds. But where there had once been neighboring homes of equal grandeur, there were now smaller houses, perhaps three or four to the land once occupied by a single dwelling. The old trees along the sidewalks remained, though, and if this neighborhood had ever gone down, it had since risen again in quality. The streets were quiet, with the new houses set back behind small and carefully manicured lawns. As he walked Guttman saw a few children playing in backyards, but it was very quiet. Not like in New York, he thought, where no matter which direction you walked, there was lots of things to see, even if they was just people. But this is nice too, he told himself. Only different.

He didn't turn when he reached the corner, deciding to extend his around-the-block stroll. It was half an hour before he approached the front entrance of the Golden Valley Center from the opposite direction, and he had made up his mind that he'd try to take this walk, a constitutional, every day. This time he found Carstairs in the library.

Guttman stood at the door for a moment, watching as Carstairs sat at the chessboard, studying the pieces and looking at a thick book.

"Mr. Carstairs, I wonder could I talk to you a minute?"

Carstairs looked up at him, then down at the book, and finally, as if it had been a difficult decision, he closed the book, adjusted his glasses, and nodded at Guttman. "Of course," he said.

"Thank you. There's a little problem," Guttman began. "It's about Mr. Cohen. I think you knew him, and I'm wondering, maybe you could help." Guttman paused, hoping for a response, but Carstairs merely looked directly at him. "I don't know if you heard what Miss Walters was saying before she died," Guttman continued. "Some people is wondering, though, maybe she was right."

"Mr. Guttman," Carstairs said slowly, "no one was . . . is more disturbed by the loss of Miss Walters than I. However, I'm afraid that the shock of . . . Mr. Cohen's passing was more than she could cope with."

"You could be right," Guttman said. "To be honest, I thought the same thing. But the point is, well, it's a little different."

"Mr. Guttman, this is a difficult time of life to be forming close relationships. Miss Walters did that, however, and it had a serious effect upon her."

"I understand that . . ."

"We've all suffered losses," Mr. Carstairs went on, "friends, family . . . If there's any consolation, I sometimes think it's that there are fewer losses left for us to endure."

"Well, you could always make new friends with young people," Guttman said, smiling. Carstairs hesitated, then smiled back, and Guttman felt a little better.

"What was it you wanted, Mr. Guttman?"

"Well, the thing is, what if, just for argument's sake, what if Cohen didn't die from natural things."

66

"I don't think that's the case, Mr. Guttman."

"But it's possible."

"And if it is?"

"Well, at first I done the same thing as you," Guttman said. "I only went and talked to Miss Walters in the first place because Mrs. Kaplan made such a fuss. And I also figured how she wasn't thinking so good. Everybody else thought the same thing, too . . ."

Guttman raised his hand to keep Carstairs from interrupting. "Dr. Morton talked to me about it, and I also saw the police detective what investigated. The thing is, Mr. Carstairs, everybody—even me, and if you'll forgive me saying it, you too—all of us started out not believing Miss Walters, because she was old. Even us, and we're old also. But it's the way people think. Automatic we decide if someone old says something that don't seem right, there's no point in paying attention. Now, I don't know from you, but I know that I don't think no different than I used to. I'm seventy-two, and physically it's not the same like thirty, forty years ago. And maybe I got different ideas than I used to, but it don't mean that my mind don't work as good, just because the body don't." Guttman paused for a moment. "Do you see what I'm getting to?"

"Yes," Carstairs said slowly. "I think so. And, I suppose, you have a point. However, all of that notwithstanding, I don't believe that Samuel Cohen died of anything other than a heart attack."

"Okay. But the thing is, some of us, we got this feeling like if we don't make sure, if we don't look into maybe there's a small possibility Miss Walters wasn't just talking crazy, then it's going to bother us a long time. So we're trying to find out," Guttman concluded.

"Why do you come to me?" Carstairs asked after a moment.

"That's the next thing. I got to ask this, so I don't want you should take offense. The thing is, they say you and Mr. Cohen had a fight. Over Miss Walters." Guttman got it out quickly, and then waited anxiously for the reaction. It was surprisingly mild.

"I think that's an exaggeration, Mr. Guttman. We argued, but we certainly didn't have a fight."

"The thing is, I heard you had the . . . argument, about Miss Walters."

"Yes," Carstairs said. "But perhaps not in the way you think. You see, Miss Walters and I had known one another for some time. We were, well, we were very good friends. I had . . . the greatest admiration, and . . . and affection for her," he said, stopping to think for a moment. "I suppose I may have felt some jealousy when Cohen began paying so much attention to her. It's ironic, really. Samuel only moved here because of me."

"Because of you? You knew him before?"

"A number of years. My firm was employed by Mr. Cohen. Over a period of some ten years, I think we became fairly good friends. Perhaps acquaintances is a better word," he added.

"And Cohen came here and took your girl friend. That must have been very hard for you," Guttman said.

"Miss Walters wasn't my girl friend. We . . ." Carstairs stopped and looked at Guttman carefully for a moment. "I think I understand. And I must say that I don't think I like it. You're here to question me, aren't you? You're here, practically accusing me of having something to do with Samuel's death."

"I'm not accusing," Guttman protested.

"I see no reason to continue this discussion." Carstairs reached for his book and started to get up.

"I got a reason for you," Guttman said. "Just suppose that something happened to Cohen, like Miss Walters said. If she was right, it could also be the same thing happened to her."

Carstairs put the book down. "Go on," he said.

"There's nothing to go on with. Except to find out." Guttman shrugged. "It's probably nothing, like you say. But a person couldn't just ignore the possibility."

"Mr. Cohen and I did argue about Miss Walters," Carstairs said after a moment. "I thought it was a mistake, their plans to be married."

"And?"

"And nothing more. I might also say, Mr. Guttman, that I did not kill Samuel Cohen. So far as I am concerned, no one did."

"But it's possible," Guttman insisted.

"Theoretically, I suppose so," Carstairs said grudgingly.

"Mr. Carstairs, do you mind if I ask a personal question?"

"You've been doing that for some time," Carstairs said. Both men smiled.

"Mr. Carstairs, I was wondering, and I know it's none of my business, but why didn't you marry Miss Walters yourself? If not here, then before, even?"

"I've been a bachelor all of my life, Mr. Guttman. It's very hard to contemplate so drastic a change in one's pattern of living at this stage," Carstairs said quietly.

"I guess so," Guttman agreed. "Mr. Carstairs, would you tell me what you know about Cohen, from before?"

"Why?"

"Because the way we figure, if anything happened to Cohen, the first thing we got to do is figure out who could've had a reason. I mean, it's the only place we got to start."

"What would you like to know?"

"Anything."

"I really don't know where to begin," Carstairs said.

"Well, I'm not so good with it myself," Guttman admitted. "But maybe I can give you some questions for a beginning. You said you knew about Cohen's business, before he retired. Maybe there's something there."

"Samuel didn't really retire from business, to be technical. He was still an officer of the company, with the title of chairman, although he stopped going to the office a year and a half ago."

"I thought he was completely retired."

"From the day-to-day operations, yes. But he still maintained an interest in the business."

"It must be a pretty big business," Guttman said.

"Moderately so. Samuel was a partner in a clothing-manufacturing firm."

"That I know something about," Guttman said. "Fifty years I was in that business. The last twenty years, the head cutter. But still, it must've been a pretty big business that he should stay as chairman. Where I worked, there was an owner, maybe two partners, that's all."

"That's more or less the way it is here, too," Carstairs said. "But when Samuel decided to retire, it wasn't practical for his partner to buy up his interest in the business. And Samuel didn't mind keeping his hand in, so to speak. Overall, I don't think there was any problem in the situation, if that's what you're driving at. Eli probably preferred this arrangement to the alternatives."

"What do you mean?"

"If Samuel had sold his interest in the company, then there would have been a new partnership. A partnership is, I suppose, like a marriage. Very few are perfect, but once you've adjusted to it, you're reluctant to change."

"This partner we're talking about, he's got a name?"

"Eli Strauss."

"So if Cohen was the chairman, this Strauss was what, the president?"

"Yes."

"And now what is he?"

"I really don't know," Carstairs said.

"If this Strauss couldn't buy Cohen's share in the business before, what's he gonna do now?"

"Mr. Guttman, are you suggesting . . . ?"

"I'm not suggesting anything. I'm only asking questions."

Carstairs thought for a moment, then nodded his head and adjusted his glasses. "You're looking for a motive, something whereby Eli Strauss would have profited from Samuel's death. Without knowing the contents of Samuel's will, I wouldn't like to speculate. However, it's customary with businesses owned by two or three people to have some kind of key-man insurance."

"Key-man insurance?"

"Generally a means of assuring that the business won't suffer financially in the event one partner dies. In some cases, there are provisions that enable the surviving partner to take over full ownership . . ."

"So it could turn out to be a motive," Guttman said. "Of course, we don't know," he added quickly. "We don't know what the arrangements is, and we don't know if maybe this

Strauss was in trouble for money, or maybe Cohen was making things hard on him . . ."

"All right, Mr. Guttman," Carstairs said resignedly.

"I'm not accusing anybody," Guttman said.

"No, but as you say, it's a possibility." Carstairs glanced at the chessboard for a moment, and his interest seemed to wander. "What do you propose to do with this possibility of yours, Mr. Guttman?" he asked.

"I don't know, exactly." Guttman took a cigar from his pocket and removed the cellophane. "The best thing, of course, would be if there was more information. Just because a person's a possibility in the beginning, that don't mean he done anything."

"You're suggesting that further investigation is in order."

"Something like that," Guttman agreed.

"And how do you propose to do that?" Carstairs asked, with a faint smile.

"Well, I don't know exactly, at the minute." Guttman lit his cigar. "I'll have to think on it. You see, in the first place, we had to find out if it was possible maybe that Mr. Cohen didn't die from a heart attack. That was the first possible to consider. Miss Brady's working on that, and she says it could've been something else."

"Margaret Brady?"

"She was head nurse here. She knows about these things, so she talked to the others, the nurse on duty when Cohen died."

"I'm surprised that she'd be a party to this," Carstairs said.

"Mr. Carstairs, we're not doing nothing wrong," Guttman said sternly.

"You're about to pry into people's personal affairs, aren't you? You've subjected me to some rather personal questions, you're seeking some way of looking into Eli Strauss' business, aren't you?"

"You could look on it that way," Guttman admitted. "But I already thought about it. You could call it snooping, sure. But a little bit of snooping isn't so important as finding out if somebody killed another person. And if not, then nobody's gonna talk about what they snooped, anyway."

"You make your point very well," Carstairs said after a moment. He looked at the chessboard again, moved a pawn, then moved it back, took his glasses off, rubbed the bridge of his nose, and finally turned his gaze back to Guttman.

"I'll help you," he said.

"I was hoping for that."

"There are conditions, however. First, I'll be the one to decide what information is pertinent. That is, if I learn something about the business, the financial situation, which has no bearing on this matter—"

"Before you say anything more, I got to interrupt. With that kind of conditions, it's better you don't get involved," Guttman said.

"Surely, Mr. Guttman, you understand—"

"Mr. Carstairs, I thought about this, too. Let's suppose somebody killed Cohen. You think that kind of person wouldn't do something again? It's possible it already happened, with Miss Walters. And here we are, asking questions. So what kind of safety is there for us?" Guttman asked.

"I hadn't considered the possibility of any danger," Carstairs admitted. "Perhaps it's because I still don't think anything happened. But I'm only referring to information which doesn't relate . . ."

"Something once happened to me in New York, and I learned a lesson. Who knows what's important? To you or me, maybe it don't seem important. But to a person what already killed someone, who knows? So what's he gonna do? He finds out you know something, it's not so good. But if there's a couple of people all knowing the same things, then it's different."

"Safety in numbers," Carstairs said.

"More than alone."

"Very well," Carstairs agreed. "But everything must be kept in strict confidence. I don't like to violate a trust."

"Everybody will keep it secret, whatever it is," Guttman promised.

"Everybody?"

"Miss Brady you know about. Also Mrs. Kaplan, Mrs. O'Rourke and Mr. Mishkin."

"That's quite a group."

"The Golden Valley Irregulars, they call it."

"Indeed," Carstairs said. "Very well. I'm not sure why I'm agreeing to this, but I'll help you."

"I know why," Guttman said.

"I wish you'd explain it to me, then."

"Because of what you said. How you was . . . friends with Miss Walters."

Guttman left Mr. Carstairs in the library and walked back to the snack lounge. Why, he wondered, after all my worrying, all of a sudden I feel so good. Except for the cold, which isn't getting better, I feel okay physically. Maybe that's from the walk. But mostly, it's because there's something to do. The whole mystery business could lead to nothing, but meanwhile, it's something to do. It's important to be finding out. And that I like. Nu, so what's wrong with that? Why shouldn't I have something that interests me? A hobby I don't got. So I'll make like a detective.

The Golden Valley Irregulars had reassembled. Guttman noticed that they had left the chair at the head of the table for him. They're sitting like a big executives' meeting in the movies, he thought. The only thing they ain't got is pads and pencils, and the bottles with water. So they got a cup of tea instead.

"Well," Mrs. Kaplan asked as he sat down, "did you find him?"

"I found him. I found him and we had a long talk." Margaret Brady looked at him quickly.

"And?" Mrs. Kaplan prompted.

"And Mr. Carstairs is gonna help," Guttman said.

"He's gonna help us?" Mrs. Kaplan exclaimed.

"Mr. Guttman, what kind of help is Mr. Carstairs going to be giving us when he's our first suspect?" Agnes O'Rourke asked.

"Good help," Guttman said. "And whether a person is a suspect or not isn't a good thing to decide so quick. If we're gonna be fair to people, we shouldn't forget that we still don't even know if anything happened. Remember that," he said sternly, looking at each in turn. He was surprised by the way they lowered their eyes.

"We ain't gonna go around accusing people of things," Guttman went on. "All we're doing is first trying to find out if something happened, and then if anybody had a reason for it happening." He paused to relight his cigar.

"You're right, Mr. Guttman," Agnes O'Rourke said. "We should be more charitable."

"We're getting ahead of ourselves," Miss Brady said.

"How is your Mr. Carstairs going to help?" Mrs. Kaplan asked. Evidently, she wasn't convinced.

"Mr. Carstairs knew Cohen from before, and his partner too," Guttman said. Then he reviewed his conversation for them. "So he's gonna see what he can find out about that part of things," he concluded.

Miss Brady seemed to look relieved.

"There's still a small problem," Mrs. Kaplan said.

"What's that?"

"Well, if Mr. Carstairs isn't a number-one suspect, he's still a suspect. He had a motive."

"So?"

"So can we rely on the information he gives us? We musn't forget—"

"I'm not forgetting," Guttman said wearily. "But you got a better way to find out about Cohen's partner, and the business? Okay," he said when she didn't answer. "So meantime, let's see what else we got to look into. Did anybody learn anything?"

"I did," Mrs. O'Rourke said, raising her hand.

"Okay, what did you learn?"

"I learned that Mr. Cohen had a nephew. And I also learned that he and his nephew didn't get on very well. As a matter of fact, I was told that they argued about his plans to marry Miss Walters," Mrs. O'Rourke recited. "The nephew's name is Cole," she added.

"Who told you all this stuff?" Guttman asked.

"Oh, that lovely couple the Bowseniors. You know them, the ones who are always together. She paints and he smokes those big cigars."

74

"Maybe you could point them out to me later," Guttman said, casually putting his cigar into the ashtray. "Does anyone else have something?" He waited, but no one answered. "Okay," he said finally. "I got a question. It's for Miss Brady, but everybody should think about it. We already learned that something could've been given to Cohen. Only we don't know when it could've been given to him." He let them think about that for a moment, and was pleased to see that they seemed to understand.

"Of course," Mrs. Kaplan said. "So far we've only looked for a motive. We haven't even thought about an alibi."

"And we'll have to know the time when the alibis are to be for," Mrs. O'Rourke added.

Both Mrs. O'Rourke and Mrs. Kaplan looked at Miss Brady.

"At the outside," Miss Brady said, "I'd say within twenty-four hours of his death. But probably less." She thought for a moment. "I think we can figure on twelve hours. But that's assuming the agent was introduced orally. If it was a hypodermic, then the whole thing could have been over in a few seconds."

"That don't help too much," Mishkin said. "Any time in twelve hours, nobody's gonna have an alibi for all that time." He shuffled the deck of cards one last time and began laying out a hand of solitaire.

"Maybe we could figure out something," Guttman said. "If it wasn't with a needle, then it was something Cohen ate, right? Okay, so if we look on the day before he died, all we got to do is find out where he was all day."

"I don't see where that's going to help us," Mrs. O'Rourke said.

"If he never left here," Miss Brady explained, "then we'd know that it was either introduced into his food here at the Center, or else it was a needle."

"And then all we'd have to do is find out which suspect was here that day," Mrs. Kaplan added.

"Well, but how are we to find out where Mr. Cohen was that day?" Mrs. O'Rourke asked.

"The same way we find out anything," Mishkin said. "Talk to people. Somebody might remember something."

"Okay, so that's best for you and Mrs. O'Rourke to do," Guttman said. "Today's Friday. You got the whole weekend you could talk to people."

"What about Miss Brady?" Agnes O'Rourke asked.

"I've got an idea of my own," she answered. "I've got some research to do. Maybe I can pin things down a little better. I'll check to see how long various drugs would have taken, whether they might have been detected in the food, and see which ones would be most likely. It'll help if we can pin the time down better."

"And Mrs. Kaplan, she's got to have something to do," Mrs. O'Rourke went on.

"I have an idea also," Dora Kaplan said. "Besides, what could I do on the weekend?"

"It's not like we got to figure this all out between now and Monday," Guttman said. "The main thing is to figure it out careful."

"Mr. Guttman's right," Mrs. Kaplan said. "We'll get him, sooner or later."

"Like the mounted police," Mrs. O'Rourke said.

Mishkin glanced at her and shook his head, just a fraction of an inch.

"There's one more thing," Guttman said, looking at his watch. "Before we go, this is something everybody got to realize. I told it to Carstairs, and now everybody else should know too. Let's everybody realize that if something happened to Cohen and Miss Walters, it could happen again. But it ain't too likely if we're smart. And that means no secrets. Anybody learns something, they got to tell somebody else."

They were silent for a moment, looking at one another, until Margaret Brady spoke. "We'll be our own insurance policy," she said.

"It ain't the kind of thing to make you sleep easy at night," Mishkin said.

"I wouldn't worry too much," Guttman reassured them. "We got one very important thing to make it safer for us."

"What's that?" Mrs. Kaplan asked.

"Nobody's gonna take us very serious when we ask questions," Guttman explained.

Waiting for Lois to pick him up, Guttman thought about how he would keep his activities secret from her. He could, of course, tell her about it and try to make it a joke. But he wasn't sure that she'd see it that way. So I just wouldn't tell her, he decided. Mrs. Kaplan's a worry, who knows what she might say to her daughter? And her daughter would tell Lois. But who's so sure Mrs. Kaplan wants her daughter knowing? Probably it's the same thing there. Okay, so stop worrying, he told himself. If it comes out, it comes out, and you'll worry then. Meantime, there's nothing you could do about it.

When Lois arrived, he realized he'd been silly to worry. His daughter loved him, but she had already forgotten his mention of Mrs. Kaplan and Miss Walters. All she could talk about was a new zoning proposal that her anti-pollution group was going to fight. That evening after dinner Guttman borrowed his grandson Joseph's copy of Sherlock Holmes stories, and because he didn't care for the television program the family was going to watch, he took it to his room. He had his own TV set, but if he was going to lead the Golden Valley Irregulars, he thought he might see how the original had been managed. Sherlock Holmes was interesting, he decided, but it wasn't going to help very much. In the first place, he read four stories without ever hearing about the Irregulars. In the second place, a Sherlock Holmes he wasn't, with looking at people's shoes to see mud, and figure out what kind of work they did by ink on their cuffs.

Saturday was a busy day. In the morning he went with Michael to watch while Joseph's Little League team practiced. Guttman stayed with his older grandson while Michael went to the other side of the park to watch David's Pee Wee team practice. In the afternoon, while the boys were at the movies and Michael and Lois were playing tennis, Guttman earned his keep by baby-sitting with Sara. Unfortunately, she slept all afternoon, but it gave him a chance to read more of Sherlock Holmes.

Sunday, after breakfast, Michael suggested a drive to the beach, and the family jumped at the idea. It wasn't Guttman's favorite way to spend a day, since he didn't swim and just sitting under the umbrella in the shade could get dull, but he didn't mind too much being outdoors. And he had his book to read. By the time he went to bed Sunday night, he had finished nearly a hundred pages of Sherlock Holmes stories, discovered that the Baker Street Irregulars or whatever were a bunch of kids, and didn't have any better idea of how to go about proving a crime had been committed, or finding the culprit, than he'd had before he started reading. Still, he enjoyed the stories, and it had been a nice weekend. Much better than in New York, where he would have sat in the park if the weather was nice, and maybe played some checkers or chess, and watched other children, grown now, come to pay a Sunday afternoon visit to their lonely parents.

They met over coffee Monday morning. Mishkin, Mrs. O'Rourke and Miss Brady were waiting for him. Guttman got some coffee and sat down to join them.

"Mrs. Kaplan isn't here yet?" he asked.

"I didn't see her," Mrs. O'Rourke answered.

"Maybe we should wait," Guttman suggested, "before you tell what you found out over the weekend."

"It wasn't much," Mishkin said. "You want to play a couple of hands of pinochle?"

Guttman looked at Miss Brady and shrugged. "I'd rather play a game of chess," he said, "but that takes longer, so I'll play pinochle."

After a few minutes Miss Brady got up and said she'd be back in a little while. Agnes O'Rourke began reading a new movie magazine. It was ten-thirty before Dora Kaplan arrived.

"I have some news," she said immediately. "That's why I'm late."

"We was waiting for you," Guttman told her. "But everybody should be here, so now we got to wait for Miss Brady."

"Where is she?"

"She was here before," Guttman said.

"Maybe she's outside," Mrs. O'Rourke suggested. "I'll go look."

They waited in silence, Mrs. Kaplan obviously anxious to tell her news and only with great effort holding herself in check.

She almost sighed with relief when she saw Mrs. O'Rourke returning with Margaret Brady in tow.

"I thought I remembered something on Friday, when we talked," Mrs. Kaplan said as soon as the other women were seated. "But I didn't want to say anything until I was sure. Well, this morning I found out. The girl who cleans for my Phyllis also cleans for Cohen's nephew's wife. So," she went on, "this morning, which is the day that Naomi comes—she's a lovely person, and so clean—I decided to wait until she came, so I could talk to her. Naomi and I get along very well, which is more than I can say for the Cole woman. Naomi tells me she's a real *kvetch*."

"What's a *kvetch*?" Mrs. O'Rourke asked.

"A complainer. Somebody who whines all the time," Mishkin explained.

"Anyway, Naomi and I had a long talk," Mrs. Kaplan resumed. "And I learned a lot about the Coles. First, what Mrs. O'Rourke told us Friday is absolutely right. Naomi told me how Mrs. Cole talked to her about Cohen, and how she was upset that he was talking about getting married again. Mrs. Cole said it was because of his age and everything, but Naomi knew better. It was the money. She could tell from things Mrs. Cole let slip. This Cole was the only relative Cohen had, and he thought he was going to be rich when his uncle died. He figured everything would come to him."

"Well, that's a good thing to know," Guttman said. "But it don't tell us too much."

"I have more," Mrs. Kaplan said, pleased with herself.

"You want we should guess?" Mishkin asked.

He was as involved as anyone else, Guttman thought, even if he did play solitaire most of the time someone was talking.

"I happen to know," Mrs. Kaplan said, "that Lawrence Cole went to see a lawyer, and a doctor, to find out if he could get his uncle declared crazy, to keep him from marrying Miss Walters."

"Crazy or incompetent?" Miss Brady asked as the others digested this new information.

"What's the difference?"

"Well, crazy, as you put it, means they might have been

trying to put him away. But incompetent," Miss Brady explained, "might just mean that the nephew wanted to be made Cohen's guardian."

"I thought guardians was only for children," Guttman said. "Like when they got no parents."

"That, too. Children because they can't take care of themselves, and older people too, sometimes, if they can prove that they're mentally incompetent. The guardian usually gets to take control over the other person's finances, and so forth. Unfortunately," she added, "senility isn't something that can really be treated with medication. Or therapy."

"So if they was trying to get him incompetent, then who would have been the guardian?" Guttman asked.

"The nephew, presumably," Miss Brady answered. "He was the only relative."

"So . . ." Guttman said. "That's very interesting. What happened?" he asked Mrs. Kaplan.

"Nothing. The lawyer told Cole he'd have to get a doctor to make a certificate, but the doctor told Cole his uncle was fine."

"Did Cohen know about this, I wonder?"

"I don't think so," Mrs. Kaplan said. "From what Naomi says, they was afraid to let him find out, because he might've taken Cole out of his will."

Guttman nodded and decided it was time for a cigar. Now they had a new suspect, and he'd have to think about it.

"I just thought of something," Mrs. O'Rourke said. "Where's Mr. Carstairs?"

"That's right, where is he?" Mrs. Kaplan added.

"He isn't here," Guttman said. "So we'll worry about it later. Now we got to think about what Mrs. Kaplan told us."

"A no-goodnik what says his uncle's crazy so he can get his money, that's what I call a good suspect," Mishkin said.

"It's a beginning," Guttman agreed. "First he fights . . . I just remembered something. Does anybody know, did Cohen make up a will?"

They looked at one another, wondering why they hadn't thought of it sooner.

82

"I'll try to check it out," Miss Brady said. "There may be something in the files on it."

"Good. So now, is there anything else?" Guttman asked.

"I've got something," Miss Brady said. "It's mostly for the people who live here, Mr. Mishkin and Mrs. O'Rourke."

"You live here too," Mishkin said.

"My arrangement is a little different. I own my cottage. But what I want to look into is what arrangements you two made when you first came to live here."

"What kind of arrangements do you got in mind?"

"Do you mean how we pay for things?" Mrs. O'Rourke asked.

"Uh huh. I know it's personal, but it's important."

"I signed a contract," Mrs. O'Rourke said. "We had a little house, not too large but very nice, and there was just a bit of cash toward the end. That's all gone, so now there's just my social security, but I signed the house over to the Center when I moved here."

"With me it was a little different," Mishkin said. "But not too much. My house also I signed over. The money I arranged a little different, with my children, but it's like with Mrs. O'Rourke."

"Right," Miss Brady said. "Now, there are two ways something like this, a residency here, can be handled. One is a monthly charge, and believe me, it's not cheap. The other is for someone moving in to sign over to the Center whatever property they own."

"I didn't know that," Guttman said.

"It's standard procedure."

Standard procedure maybe, Guttman thought. But if it was me, I wouldn't've had nothing to sign over. I couldn't've lived in a place like this. So why did I never think about it, back in New York? What's the matter, Guttman, did you think you'd always be able to live by yourself and take care without help?

"What's the point of this?" Mrs. Kaplan asked Miss Brady, interrupting his thoughts.

"Okay, I'll tell you. I got to wondering about this over the weekend, and I checked out the billing procedures. Mr. Cohen was paying a flat monthly rate. I guess he could afford to. But Miss Walters had signed one of those contracts, and it provided that any property she owned, plus anything she might come in to, would go to the Center upon her death." Miss Brady took a moment to look at each of them. "Now," she continued, "if Cohen had married her, and then died, under California law, everything he had would have gone over to her, unless he made out a will that specified otherwise."

"And when she died, the Center would get it all," Mrs. Kaplan said. "That's very interesting."

"But of course, if Cohen died before he was married, all bets was off," Mishkin said.

"And if the nephew, this Cole, knew about it . . ." Mrs. Kaplan said.

"It makes for a pretty strong motive," Miss Brady agreed.

"Okay," Guttman said. "So now we got a new question for the nephew. We got to find out if he knew about this. We also got to find out about a will, because maybe there was one that gave money to the nephew, and he could've known about that, too. And that would mean he wouldn't've worried about his uncle getting married."

"But he did worry about that," Mrs. O'Rourke said.

"I think we'll have to pay a call on Mr. Cole," Mrs. Kaplan said with quiet determination.

Pay a call? Oy, Guttman thought. "There's something I'd like to find out first," he said. "I'd like to find out about the poison that could've been given, what we talked about last week. Maybe if we know what times we're talking about, it would help when we talk to the nephew. Also, maybe it would be a good idea to talk to the wife first."

"Why not just face him with the facts?" Mrs. O'Rourke asked.

"Because from what Mrs. Kaplan tells us, we know the wife talks a lot. So maybe she'll tell us something it would help."

"So the first thing," Mishkin said slowly, "is to find out about Cohen's last day. I didn't mean it that way," he added as they fell silent.

"That's what we got to finish up first," Guttman said. "So who was this couple you talked to, Mrs. O'Rourke? The ones what knew about the nephew."

"The Bowseniors."

It wasn't until after lunch that Guttman met the Bowseniors. Mrs. O'Rourke pointed them out to him during lunch, and afterward he went looking for them. They were outside on the lawn, sitting in the shade and reading. Guttman felt reluctant to disturb them, but decided there was no point in waiting. Too much information was being gathered by his Irregulars, and he had to see whether he could make sense of it.

"Excuse me," he said, standing over them. "Is you Mr. and Mrs. Bowsenior?"

"Jay Bowsenior," the man said, standing up and offering his hand.

"I'm Max Guttman."

"Pleasure to meet you. This is my wife, Ursula." Mr. Bowsenior was of medium height and build, wearing a white shirt and a tie and a cardigan sweater. His wife, an energetic-looking woman, smiled up at Guttman.

"How do you do?" he said.

"We wondered when you were going to get around to us," Mr. Bowsenior said.

"You was expecting me?"

"After that talk we had with Agnes, we thought you might stop by," Mrs. Bowsenior said. "Please sit down."

Guttman drew up a lawn chair and adjusted it so that he was facing the two of them. "How come you figured I'd be talking to you?"

"Well, you're in charge of the investigation, aren't you?" Mr. Bowsenior said.

"It's not exactly an investigation . . ."

"We assumed that after you'd heard from Agnes, you'd want to question us yourself," Mr. Bowsenior continued.

"To be honest, I'm not sure," Guttman said, with a small smile. "Mrs. O'Rourke told me everything, so there wasn't no point at first."

"But now there is?" Mrs. Bowsenior asked.

"It could be, yes."

"Anything we can do to help, just ask," Mr. Bowsenior said. "We've thought about this, and if anyone actually did something, that is, if Mr. Cohen was killed, well, it's as if they hurt someone in our own family."

"We were rather fond of Samuel," Mrs. Bowsenior added.

"Was you very close to him?"

"Not terribly, but we liked him. And what harms one of us, in a way, harms all of us," Mrs. Bowsenior said.

"I see."

"Would you like a cigar?" Mr. Bowsenior asked, offering Guttman one from a metal case.

"Thanks, but I just finished one."

"Take it for later, then. Bought a whole load of them couple of years ago, have them stored for me in a place downtown, my own humidor. Only trouble is I bought so many of them, I'm not sure I'll have time to smoke them all. Dr. Morton wants me to cut down on them."

"He told me the same thing," Guttman said.

"I think he tells that to everyone."

"Well, it isn't the best thing for you," Mrs. Bowsenior said.

"I think all the doctor is interested in is keeping the ashtrays clean," her husband answered, with a chuckle.

"What I wanted to talk to you about," Guttman said, "is maybe if you remember something from the day before Cohen died."

"The day before?"

"It's a long story to explain, but it could be important. I

figured since you was friends with him, maybe you'd remember."

"First thing we have to do is remember just what day it was," Mr. Bowsenior said. "Around here, someone dying isn't all that unusual, you know."

"We try to ignore it, Mr. Guttman," Mrs. Bowsenior said. "Jay has a tendency to joke about it, but then again, he jokes about everything. But most of us try to ignore reality."

"There must be half a dozen in the hospital now, ready to kick off at any moment," her husband said. "It's a wonder they don't have a separate section, kind of a death row." He lit his cigar carefully. "Well, let's see, the day before . . ."

The Bowseniors talked quietly to each other for a moment, checking dates and events until they were sure they had it right in their minds.

"We had lunch with him," Mrs. Bowsenior said. "I remember it was the day they tried to tell us the filet of sole wasn't just plain flounder."

"Right. That was the day he was so mad at his nephew. We told Mrs. O'Rourke about it."

"Did they have a fight?" Guttman asked.

"They were always fighting. No, as I recall, Sam had a big blow-up with him a week or so before, but he was still steaming."

"That was when they was fighting about Mr. Cohen getting married, right?"

"Uh huh. Nephew didn't like the idea."

"Do you know why?"

"I think it was the money," Mrs. Bowsenior said.

"Sure. He expected Sam to leave it all to him, and he knew Sam wasn't too healthy. But with Sam getting married, well, I guess the little S.O.B. was disappointed, to put it mildly."

"Watch your language, dear," Mrs. Bowsenior reprimanded.

"You call him that like you know him," Guttman said. "Did you ever meet him?"

"Once, when he stopped by to talk to Sam. Seemed nice

enough, if you didn't look too closely," Mr. Bowsenior said. "Can't say that I have anything against him personally, to be fair about it. Just what Sam told us."

"So you had lunch with Cohen that day, right? Do you know was he here all that day?"

"No, as a matter of fact, he was out in the afternoon. Left a little after lunch. But he was around in the evening. We played some backgammon."

"Did you have dinner with him?" Guttman asked.

"No, we like to be by ourselves at dinner," Mrs. Bowsenior said. "We see so many people during the day."

"And we're involved in just about every evening activity," her husband added. "Bridge tournaments, lectures, you name it."

"That's nice," Guttman said. "Well, I want to thank you very much."

"Have we helped?"

"A lot, I think. The only thing," he added, with a smile, "is since I'm not so sure what I'm doing, it's hard for me always to know what helps and what doesn't. But it was nice talking to you."

"Come back any time. We're always around. Do you play backgammon, by the way?" Mr. Bowsenior asked.

"No, I don't." Guttman didn't know what it was, and so he was quite sure he didn't play it. "What I'd like to play sometime, to be honest, is bocce."

"What's that?" Mrs. Bowsenior asked.

"It's sort of an Italian lawn bowls," her husband explained.

"Did you ever play?" Guttman asked.

"Years and years ago. Do you play?"

"No, but I always wanted to. Well, not always, but for a couple of years. In New York, I used to watch them play in the park. Maybe we could get somebody to make up a court here," he said.

"It's a good idea. I'll present it to the council," Mr. Bowsenior said. "Be kind of fun, since I can't stand croquet, and I'm not up to ping-pong any more."

"The council?"

"Residents' council. We meet once a week. Usually no one attends, since nothing happens."

"It would be nice if they could do it," Guttman said.

"I'll see what I can do," Mr. Bowsenior promised.

Guttman thanked them again and walked back toward the main building. It was past two now, and with only two and a half hours left to the afternoon, he knew that he wouldn't be going to see Cohen's nephew, or his wife, today. And there really wasn't anything to tell the group that couldn't wait until morning. But if he went back to the snack lounge, they'd be there, and he'd have to discuss the case with them. He went to the library instead, hoping to find Miss Brady there, or Mr. Carstairs. A game of chess might be nice.

The library was empty, which meant he could either sit and read, or relent and play pinochle and discuss the case. He found a magazine that he hadn't seen and went back outside to sit in the shade and watch a slow game of croquet. Surprisingly, he wasn't disturbed all afternoon. It was only later, as he waited out front for Lois, that he remembered it was oil-painting day, and Dora Kaplan had discovered an unsuspected talent. Mrs. O'Rourke, of course, was in the class, too.

When the family had finished dinner, and the boys had been sent to their room to do their homework, Michael made his announcement.

"I've got to go up to San Francisco this weekend," he said.

"When do you have to leave?" Lois asked.

"I've got some meetings on Friday, probably run all day, but I think I'll be able to take the morning flight."

"Then you'll be able to get back Friday?"

"Well, I was thinking that maybe the two of us might stay over a couple of days."

"What do you mean?" Lois asked.

"Oh, just that it would be nice for us to get away by ourselves for a while," Michael said. "We haven't spent much time alone in quite a while . . ."

"Oh, darling, I don't see how we can," Lois began.

"Sure you do. Joseph and David can stay with the Stones, and I'm sure Marjorie wouldn't mind taking care of the baby for a day or two . . ."

"Oh, Michael, it would be so nice, but I just don't know . . ."

"Come on, we've taken care of Marjorie's baby more than once. She owes us."

"I wasn't thinking of that so much, but . . . Can we afford it?"

"Can't afford not to," Michael said. "Couple of days by ourselves will put the bloom back in your cheeks."

"Well . . ." Lois hesitated, and suddenly Guttman realized that she was looking at him sideways. "Maybe we'll talk about it later," she said.

"We'll talk about it now," Michael said, looking at his father-in-law. "If you're worrying about Pop, you're being silly. He took good care of himself before he came here, and—"

"Absolutely," Guttman said. "What's the problem? I can't fix a meal for myself? Okay, so I don't drive the car. So if I want to go somewhere, there's a bus. Besides, where do I go, anyway? You could leave food in the house, I'll be fine."

"Oh, I wasn't worrying about that, Pop," Lois said quickly.

Guttman looked at Michael and shrugged. He felt close to his son-in-law, and now he realized that part of the reason was that Michael never treated him like a child. Michael treated him like an equal. And, Guttman thought, with most people, when you got old, you wasn't really an equal to them any more.

"So if you're not worrying about that, what's the problem?" Guttman asked his daughter.

"Well, we'll see," she said.

"Michael, would you excuse me a minute? I got something to say to my daughter, maybe it would be better if we're alone."

Michael looked at him, smiled just a bit, and went out of the kitchen.

"Sit down, Lois," Guttman said.

"Pop . . ."

"Please," he insisted. Lois sighed, but she sat down across the table from him. "Now," he began, "do you remember when you was always asking me to come here with you, and I was always saying no?"

"Of course, but—"

"Let me finish," Guttman said firmly. "Now, why do you think I was always saying no? You think I didn't want to see you? You think I didn't want to be with the *kindele?*" He raised his hand to keep her from interrupting. "No, that's not why. I was always saying no because I didn't want I should be messing into your life. I didn't want I should be a burden."

"You're not a burden," Lois said. "Honestly, Pop . . ."

"And I'm not gonna be one, either," Guttman agreed. "Michael, thank God, makes a good income, so even if with my pension and the social security there wasn't enough to cover, I know the extra wouldn't be a big problem. I also know, with the Center, maybe it costs a little more than you tell me—" He had to raise his hand again to keep her from speaking.

"Okay, so with the money there's no problem," he continued. "Not that I don't appreciate. Believe me, I do. I like going to the Center. It's good to have people to talk to every day. Also, it's good to be here with you, and Michael, and the children. But there's still a question about being a burden. And if you're going to say, 'No, I can't do something because of Pop,' then I'm a burden." Guttman paused for breath, but Lois didn't try to interrupt now.

"Lois, I know you love me, and I know you worry. I worry about you, too, if something's wrong. But nothing's wrong with me. A baby I'm not. And, thank God, I'm not a sick person in bed all the time. So I don't want you should be worrying so much you couldn't even go away for a weekend. It's important to me," he added.

After a moment Lois looked at him and smiled. Guttman thought there might be a tear in her eyes. "Okay, Pop," she said. "You've made your point. You're right, and I'm . . . I was wrong."

"So you'll go with Michael?"

"If we can dump the kids on someone, yes."

"Good," Guttman said. "After all, it would give me a chance to watch whatever I want on the color TV."

"Is it okay if I call while we're away?"

"You called when I was in New York, didn't you? Did I ever say no?"

"Okay, Pop," Lois said, getting up and giving him a hug.

"Okay," Guttman agreed. "So now you could tell Michael it's okay he could come back in the kitchen. And maybe I could have some more tea?" he asked, taking a cigar from his pocket.

Lois dropped him at the corner the next morning, and as he always did, Guttman watched her make the turn and drive off before he crossed the street to the Center.

"Mr. Guttman. I'm glad you're here."

It was Mr. Carstairs, wearing a dark-blue suit with a white shirt and dark tie. He looks younger, Guttman thought. Less like a retired person.

"We was looking for you yesterday, Mr. Carstairs," Guttman said.

"I was downtown all day. That's why I waited this morning. The next bus will be along in a moment, so there isn't much time for me to explain."

"So I won't interrupt," Guttman promised.

"Yesterday I went to my office, that is, my former office. I wanted to talk to the man who's handling the books for Fancy Fair."

"That's Cohen's old business?"

"Yes. Unfortunately, he was out at another client's, and I waited most of the day."

"Did he tell you anything?"

"I only had a moment with him," Mr. Carstairs said. "However, I'm going now to review some of our copies of recent reports with him."

"That'll help?"

"Well, Fred Blount—he's the man who's handling Fancy

94

Fair now, most of my old accounts, in fact—he'll be there, and he can fill me in if necessary."

"It sounds like a lot of work," Guttman said, not at all sure that it was.

"I enjoy it," Carstairs answered quickly.

Guttman didn't think he'd particularly enjoy returning to his old trade, even for a day or two, but he thought he could understand. "They wouldn't think it's funny, you going in like this?" he asked.

"Not at all. I help out a bit at tax time with some of the accounts I'm familiar with. I like to keep my hand in. However, I haven't looked at Fancy Fair for some time." Carstairs turned to see if the bus was coming.

"If you're sure it isn't too much work . . ."

"Not at all. I even offered to work on the books at the Center, but Dr. Morton said it wouldn't be right. I helped Dr. Aiken, you know. But of course, the arrangement was different then. He had an interest in the Center."

"I think Miss Brady said something about it. Will you be back in the afternoon to tell us what you find out?"

"I hope so. If not, then certainly first thing in the morning."

"Fine," Guttman said. "I'll tell the others."

"There's nothing to tell them yet."

"Well, you know, they figure they should know everything, even if there's nothing to know. And . . ."

"And?"

"And to be perfectly honest, well, there's still a feeling, for some people, that you didn't like Cohen, and . . ."

Mr. Carstairs looked at him for a moment, then adjusted his glasses on the bridge of his nose and nodded. "Do you feel that way, Mr. Guttman?"

"No," Guttman said. It was only later that he wondered whether he should dismiss Mr. Carstairs as a suspect so easily. Just because a person seems sincere doesn't mean they are, he thought.

The rest of the Golden Valley Irregulars were gathered around their usual table. Guttman thought they looked a little restless as he approached.

"Nu, Guttman, so where were you yesterday?" Mrs. Kaplan asked. "All afternoon, there's no Guttman."

"You was with the oil painting, wasn't you?" he asked in return. "So I didn't go no place. I was here. I was just thinking."

"Then have you figured it all out already, Mr. Guttman?" Agnes O'Rourke asked.

Guttman wondered whether the good-natured Mrs. O'Rourke was spending too much time with Mrs. Kaplan. "I just saw Mr. Carstairs," he said.

"Another one we don't see," Mrs. Kaplan said.

"He's busy," Guttman explained, telling them of Mr. Carstairs' labors. They didn't seem very impressed.

"I don't think we're making much progress," Mrs. Kaplan said.

"You're in a big hurry?" Guttman asked. "This is a half-hour television show, we got to find out what happened before the commercial? I'll tell you what, if you're in such a big hurry, you do it by yourself," he snapped, surprised at his own anger.

"No one meant anything like that, Mr. Guttman," Agnes O'Rourke said quickly.

"I'm sorry," Guttman said.

"I suppose we're all on edge," Mrs. Kaplan conceded.

Guttman glanced at Miss Brady, who seemed slightly amused. "This isn't like we was experts in what we're doing," he said. "We got to do things slow, because if we're gonna be honest, nobody is so sure what we're doing in the first place." No one answered him, and after a moment Guttman continued. "Okay," he said. "So now it's time we should talk to some of the people what's involved." He told them of his conversation with the Bowseniors, and when Cohen had, and had not, been at the Center.

"That means that Cohen could have been poisoned, if that's what happened, any time at all during the afternoon," Miss Brady said. "It's not much help, is it?"

"Well, it would be interesting if we could know who Cohen saw after he had lunch with the Bowseniors," Guttman said. "That would be something. At least, maybe we could get an alibi for someone, or not."

"Well, there's only one way to find out," Mrs. Kaplan said. "We have to go see the people."

"Who will we start with?" Mrs. O'Rourke asked.

"I was thinking about the nephew and his wife," Guttman said. "The only problem is how we're gonna get to see them. I don't think it's such a good idea to knock on the door and say I want to talk to you because your uncle might've been murdered."

"I've been thinking about that too," Mrs. Kaplan said. "As it happens, my Phyllis is chairman of the Hadassah theatre group, and I'm helping her with it."

"What's the Hadassah?" Mrs. O'Rourke asked.

"A charity group," Mishkin explained. "A bunch of women go around collecting money for Israel and stuff all the time. Your daughter's a chairman?" he asked Mrs. Kaplan.

"Two years in a row," she answered proudly.

"How come a chairman?" Mishkin teased. "How come not a chairperson, like with the political convention? Your daughter don't like women's lib?"

"Chairman, chairperson, she's in charge," Mrs. Kaplan said.

"The question is," Guttman interrupted, "how do we get to see the nephew and his wife."

"That's what I'm telling you," Mrs. Kaplan said. "Mrs. Cole is also a member of the Hadassah, and I'm helping my daughter with the tickets, so I could just go and see her that way. And when I'm there, I can question her."

"It sounds like a fine idea to me," Mrs. O'Rourke said.

"How do you know she's going to be home?" Miss Brady asked.

"Ah," Mrs. Kaplan said and smiled, "I know because today's the day Naomi cleans for her, and she told me that Mrs. Cole never goes out of the house when she's there. Naomi says maybe she doesn't trust her, but she should worry, that's her problem, not Naomi's."

Guttman thought about that for a moment, then sighed. "Okay," he said. "So we'll try it. I'll go with Mrs. Kaplan to see her after lunch."

"Why not go now?" Mrs. O'Rourke asked.

"Because," Guttman said, looking at his watch, "it's late enough already. There's more time after lunch. And it gives more time to figure out the questions to ask."

"All right," Mrs. Kaplan agreed. "We'll go first thing after lunch. I even brought some of the tickets with me. After all, she could want to buy some."

The group relaxed then, and Guttman got up and went out to the patio. He really did want some time to try to think of questions, but even more, he needed the time to accept the idea that he was actually going to go out and talk to a total stranger about a possible murder. He sat down and stared across the lawn, not really watching the croquet game, and smoked a cigar.

"Things seem to be progressing nicely," Miss Brady said, startling him. He hadn't seen her approaching.

"I'm not so sure," he answered.

"What's wrong?"

"It's not that something's wrong, it's just that I'm not so sure anything's right."

"I guess that makes sense. Actually, I just stopped by to see if you felt like playing chess."

"That would be very nice," Guttman told her. But it wasn't. He played badly, unable to concentrate, and lost three games. What was worse, though, was that he was sure that Miss Brady didn't enjoy playing, either.

After lunch Guttman stalled as long as he could, but finally, at two o'clock, he could put it off no longer, and he and Mrs. Kaplan left on their journey. For a moment Guttman thought she was going to take his arm, but she didn't. Still, she walked right onto the bus, when it came, and left him to pay the fare for both of them, which caught him by surprise. Fortunately, he had enough change. They had to take two buses, and Mrs. Kaplan talked most of the way. She wanted to work out the strategy, she explained, and they should have signals about what to say and what not to say, like when people were playing bridge.

"You just talk about the Hadassah thing," Guttman told her. "And I'll ask the questions."

That didn't sit very well with Mrs. Kaplan. "What if I think of something to ask?" she demanded.

"We could worry about it later," Guttman said. "But sometimes it's better not to ask, so people don't know what you're thinking."

"But it could be something important," she persisted.

"I tell you what," Guttman suggested. "If you let me ask the questions now, then if we need to go back, it'll be easier for you. If we both ask, maybe later she wouldn't want to talk to either one of us." Guttman had no plans to talk to Mrs. Cole twice, but it was enough, hopefully, to placate Mrs. Kaplan.

The Coles lived in a split-level ranch house, separated from the street by some forty or fifty feet of well-manicured grass. Guttman wondered whether there was as much space in the back. He was pleased that Lois and Michael had a backyard where the children could play and they could have barbecues.

"Are you sure this is the right house?" he asked as Mrs. Kaplan marched up the walk.

"Of course. I've been here before."

"I didn't know you was so friendly with them."

"Friendly I'm not. It was a charity luncheon," she answered, leading him to the front door. The house was bigger than Lois and Michael's. Cole must be doing pretty good, Guttman thought, to live like this.

When the door opened Guttman hung back and let Mrs. Kaplan do the talking. It took only a moment, and then he followed her inside, getting his first look at Mrs. Cole as he did.

"This is Mr. Guttman," Mrs. Kaplan explained. "He came to keep me company."

"How do you do?" Mrs. Cole said.

She was in her late thirties, turning a bit plump but still with a good figure, Guttman noticed. She was wearing slacks and a white blouse, with sandals on her bare feet, and she had several bracelets on each wrist. They jangled when she moved her arms. Guttman wondered whether the blond hair was dyed.

Mrs. Cole asked them to sit down, and when Mrs. Kaplan chose the chocolate-brown sofa, Guttman moved to sit in a matching easy chair. It was too soft, and as he sank back he wondered whether he'd be able to get up. Still, once you got into it, he thought, it was very comfortable. The rest of the furniture was similar—dark colors, oversized and obviously expensive. The living room walls were stucco, an off-white, and the stone floor was covered with several Indian patterned rugs. It don't get so cold out here even in winter, Guttman thought, so you could have a floor like this. In New York you'd freeze in winter. There you needed linoleum or carpets. There was a large fireplace against the wall opposite the couch, but having no experience with fireplaces, Guttman couldn't tell whether it would work or not.

Mrs. Kaplan said thank you, she would like a cup of tea, and Guttman, annoyed, said no, thank you. He didn't want to start bothering with tea. He wanted to get it over with. It took Mrs. Kaplan half a cup of tea, and several moments of chatter about mutual friends in Hadassah, to begin her pitch. As he listened, Guttman decided that she must have done this many times before. She was very good at it, and by the time Mrs. Cole asked about the price of the tickets, you knew she was sold.

"It's thirty dollars for two, but most of it's deductible," Mrs. Kaplan told her. "Hadassah gets six dollars on each one, so that's the part you can put on your taxes."

Twelve dollars out of thirty wasn't quite "most," but Guttman said nothing.

"I'm not sure I have enough cash," Mrs. Cole said. "Would a check be all right?"

"Of course. It's better for your taxes, too. It's like a receipt," Mrs. Kaplan said and smiled.

Mrs. Cole got up and went to get her purse, which was on a small table near the front door. She came back, wrote out a check, and handed it to Mrs. Kaplan.

"It's a wonderful show. I saw the reviews, from New York," Mrs. Kaplan said. "Incidentally, maybe you got some friends who'd like to go too. You could make your own party out of it."

"Well, I'm not sure."

"I tell you what. I got some extra tickets with me, right next to yours, so I'll leave you . . . six, and you could talk to your friends and see."

"I don't know if I can sell that many of them, Mrs. Kaplan," Mrs. Cole protested.

"So if you don't sell, give me a call in a week or so, or else call Phyllis, and we'll get them back. It's for a good cause, you know."

"Well, all right . . ."

"Marvelous," Mrs. Kaplan said, reaching into her purse to put the check away and select the seats from what looked to Guttman like a rather large stack of tickets. "These are very good seats, too," she explained. "I like to give the best to my customers."

"I'm sure we'll enjoy the show," Mrs. Cole said, looking not at all sure.

Then Guttman realized that Mrs. Kaplan was looking at him, and that the time had come. "Mrs. Cole," he said, "I wanted to say, while I'm here, that I'm very sorry about your uncle, your husband's uncle, Mr. Cohen."

"Did you know him?" Mrs. Cole asked.

"Not so well, but still, it must've been a shock to you," Guttman said.

"No, not really . . ."

"No? But one day he's fine, then all of a sudden . . . And you saw him just that afternoon, too," Guttman said, noticing that Mrs. Kaplan's eyes opened wider as he spoke.

"No, I didn't see Uncle Sam . . ."

"Somebody said that afternoon he came to visit you," Guttman suggested. "I don't remember who."

"No," Mrs. Cole said. "I hadn't seen him for, oh, I guess two weeks before that." She shook her head, then brightened. "Oh, I know what it must have been. Lawrence, my husband, saw his uncle that day. But it was at the office, so I didn't see him."

"That must've been it," Guttman agreed. "But still, I guess it was a big shock to your husband, seeing how he was the only relative. They must've been close."

"Well, naturally," Mrs. Cole said. "It was very sad. But we were prepared, in a way. He hadn't been well for some time, you know."

"I heard about it," Guttman said. "I wonder, could you tell me, was he, Mr. Cohen, upset about anything lately?"

"As I said, I hadn't seen him in several weeks," Mrs. Cole said, her tone growing cooler.

"I was thinking, maybe your husband told you . . ."

"I don't really know that this is . . . Why are you asking me about this, Mr. Guttman?"

"Well, it's a little hard to explain. But I'll be perfectly honest with you." He saw Mrs. Kaplan's mouth open, and he went ahead quickly before she could interrupt. "The thing is, some of the people at the Center was upset by this, you know. Mr. Cohen was very popular there. Anyway, I was just thinking, as long as I was coming here to keep Mrs. Kaplan company, maybe I could tell them about it, it might make them feel better."

"I still don't understand," Mrs. Cole said.

"Well, maybe I shouldn't put it this way, because I'm not exactly a teen-ager myself, but with some old people, well, sometimes they get funny ideas . . ." He smiled as if he was embarrassed, and wondered how he could manage such a good performance when what he was saying bothered him so much.

"Yes, I suppose so . . ." Mrs. Cole said slowly.

"So he wasn't upset or nothing, was he?"

"No . . . Well, you know, Mr. Guttman, just personal . . . family matters. We were concerned about his plans to get married again, after all these years . . ."

"It's none of my business," Guttman said, "but could I ask you why?"

"All that woman was interested in was Uncle Sam's money," she said angrily. "And at his age, well, forgive me, but there wasn't really any reason for them to get married, was there?"

"I wouldn't know," Guttman said, more to himself than to her. "You mention the money," he added. "I thought he was trying to make an arrangement to give the money to the Golden Valley Center, not to her . . ."

"Our attorney . . ." Mrs. Cole stopped herself. "Is there anything else, Mr. Guttman?"

"No, I guess not," Guttman said. "You know about Miss Walters dying, don't you?"

"I . . . No, I hadn't heard," she said.

Guttman didn't believe her. "Yes. She just got very depressed and died," he said.

"How sad."

Guttman wondered whether she meant it. "It just occurred to me," he said, "if the money was supposed to go to the Center, how could she be marrying your uncle for it?"

"It was the damned insurance—"

This time Mrs. Cole wasn't going to cooperate any more. She had caught herself twice, and, Guttman knew, he couldn't get her talking again. "I want to thank you very much," he said quickly. "I'm sure the people at the Center will be glad to hear Cohen, well, he died without problems."

"Yes," Mrs. Cole said.

They left as quickly as they could. Somehow, Mrs. Kaplan kept her peace until they reached the corner. But not a second longer.

"How could you talk like that?" she demanded. "You just went right ahead and started asking about Cohen, getting her suspicious, and—"

"I decided I wanted her suspicious," Guttman answered, slowing his pace a bit so that Mrs. Kaplan could keep up with him.

"You wanted her suspicious? But—"

"She said she didn't see Cohen for a couple of weeks, right?" Mrs. Kaplan opened her mouth to agree. Guttman continued. "But her husband saw him the same day he died. So that means we got to talk to the husband, right?"

"We were going to do that, anyway."

"Uh huh. But how could we just go see him without him getting suspicious? After we talked with his wife? Impossible."

"Mr. Guttman, I don't understand," Mrs. Kaplan admitted, shaking her head. "What does one thing have to do with the other?"

"We already know that Cole, the nephew, saw his uncle, right? So what else we got to ask him about? Could we just say, 'Did you kill your uncle?' No. So now he's gonna know we was talking to his wife, he's gonna know maybe we're trying to make something from this, and if he's guilty of something, he's gonna worry. And," he added, "we'll be able to find out how upset he is when we get to talk to him," Guttman concluded, hoping it made sense.

"I'm not sure that makes sense," Mrs. Kaplan said.

"It makes sense to me," Guttman told her.

Agnes O'Rourke was waiting near the front door when they returned to the Center. "I was afraid you wouldn't get back before they came to pick you up," she said. "So I thought I'd wait here and make an excuse, so they wouldn't worry."

"That was very thoughtful," Guttman said.

"We had a long wait for the bus coming back," Mrs. Kaplan explained.

"Did you learn anything?"

"Mr. Guttman seems to be the only one who knows," Mrs. Kaplan said.

"What do you mean?"

"Ask him."

"Are the others inside?" Guttman asked. "Did Mr. Carstairs come by, by any chance?"

"I didn't see him. I don't think he's really trying to help, Mr. Guttman," Agnes O'Rourke said.

"How about the others?"

"Mishkin is there, but I don't know where Miss Brady went."

"Okay, since it's time to leave already, you tell Mishkin we'll talk about things in the morning. Miss Brady, too. Tell them it's important."

"You learned something important, besides that Cohen saw his nephew?" Mrs. Kaplan asked.

"I learned something what could help," Guttman said. "But we got to get some more facts before we find out if it's important." Fortunately, a horn honked outside. It was Phyllis, coming to get her mother, and Guttman watched Mrs. Kaplan leave with a great sense of relief. He saw Lois arriving and went out to meet her.

"I saw you talking to Mrs. Kaplan when I pulled up," Lois

said as she pulled away from the curb. Guttman didn't answer. "She's really a lovely person," Lois commented.

"Very nice."

"Do you like her?"

"Like her?" Guttman asked suspiciously.

"Well, you know. Phyllis tells me she's always talking about you."

"Who, Phyllis?"

"Mrs. Kaplan, Pop," Lois said, smiling. "And don't be coy with me."

"Coy I don't know."

"All right," Lois said. "But one thing you have to promise. If there's anything going on between you and Mrs. Kaplan, I don't want Phyllis to have to tell me about it."

"What should be going on?" Guttman asked, alarmed.

"That's what I'm asking you."

"There's nothing going on," Guttman said firmly. And then, as if to emphasize his annoyance, Guttman lit a cigar, filling the car with acrid smoke. Lois didn't like him smoking in the car, but this time she had earned it. Mrs. Kaplan was a nice person, in her way, but anything else just hadn't entered Guttman's mind. And now that Lois had asked, he knew it wasn't going to be something he wanted to think about. Oy, he thought, one minute I'm a baby she don't want to leave alone in the house, and the next minute this. Women!

The baby knocked over her cereal bowl at breakfast the next morning, the phone rang, and Lois had to make two phone calls to rearrange the pickup schedule for the boys after school, and Michael couldn't find the cuff links he wanted to wear. Consequently, Lois asked nothing about Mrs. Kaplan on the ride to the Center, and Guttman was twenty minutes later than usual.

From the looks of the group around the table, another five minutes might have spelled disaster. Guttman got a cup of coffee and went to join them. They weren't talking, Mishkin wasn't even playing solitaire. Mrs. O'Rourke had a movie magazine, but it was lying closed in her lap. Mr. Carstairs, sitting quite still at one end of the table next to Miss Brady, seemed to be the cause of the tension. Guttman sat down, stirred sugar into his coffee, lit a cigar, and wondered whether anything had happened yet.

"Good morning," he said. They nodded. It's too big a group, he thought. Still, there's nothing to do about it now. "Miss Brady, I got something for you to check, if you could take a look at the records again." Since socializing didn't seem in order, he'd go right to business. "It could be that Cohen made out his insurance to Miss Walters before he died. It might be interesting to find out."

"I don't know if that would be in the records," Miss Brady told him.

"Well, if he did, and Miss Walters had nobody else, maybe

she wrote something turning that over to the home, like you said, when she died. It could be in the records."

"Is it important?"

"I don't know, but Mrs. Cole mentioned it yesterday. She knew about Cohen turning his money over to the Center, but she started to say something about the insurance, so I figure we ought to find out if we can."

"I'll check it as soon as I can."

"Thank you." Guttman looked at the others, and was relieved to see that Mishkin was getting ready to play solitaire again. Some people, maybe the Greeks, got beads they play with when they don't have nothing else to do, he thought. So with Mishkin it's solitaire. "Next is Mr. Carstairs," he now announced.

"Mr. Guttman, I'd prefer to discuss this in private," Carstairs said softly.

"We don't have any secrets here, Mr. Carstairs," Agnes O'Rourke said quickly.

"That's what concerns me, Mrs. O'Rourke," Carstairs answered.

"I explained at the beginning," Guttman said. "We got to trust each other with secrets. That's the way it is."

"Except for Mr. Guttman," Dora Kaplan whispered under her breath, just loud enough for Guttman to hear.

"The information I had access to is confidential, and . . ." Carstairs looked at the others.

"We're all keeping whatever secrets we get," Guttman said. "And if something don't have nothing to do with what we're looking for, then who we got to talk to about it, anyway?"

Mr. Carstairs didn't look convinced, but he adjusted his glasses and glanced down at a small notebook in his hand. "Rather than give you all of the specific figures, I'll summarize what we have," he began.

"Don't you think we'll be understanding the figures?" Mrs. O'Rourke asked.

"It's faster this way," Guttman said quickly. "Besides, Mr. Carstairs is the expert, so we'll hear it the way he says it."

"Thank you," Carstairs said, looking at Mrs. O'Rourke. "I

spent quite a bit of time yesterday going over the recent data on Fancy Fair, and I found that—"

"What's Fancy Fair?" Mrs. O'Rourke demanded.

"That's the business Cohen had, with a partner," Guttman explained.

"Thank you."

"You're welcome. Go ahead, Mr. Carstairs."

"Thank you. Over the past two years Fancy Fair has had some financial difficulties . . ."

"Ahah," Mishkin whispered.

"But of late they seem to be getting over the problems. Overall, the business is in reasonably good financial condition, although the capital position isn't as strong as I'd like to see it. The cash flow—"

"What's the capital position?" Mrs. O'Rourke asked.

"How much money they got," Mishkin told her.

"Thank you, Mr. Mishkin."

"You're welcome, Mrs. O'Rourke."

"Mr. Carstairs, could you tell just how bad they might need cash?" Mrs. Kaplan asked. "If they got bills they can't pay, for example?"

"I'll have to take a careful look at their books," Mr. Carstairs answered.

"Could you do that?"

"I plan to. Today, as a matter of fact."

"Really?" Mrs. O'Rourke inquired. "How could you arrange that, Mr. Carstairs?"

"I took the liberty of making an appointment for Mr. Guttman and myself, with Eli Strauss, for eleven-thirty this morning."

"This Eli Strauss is Cohen's partner?" Mrs. Kaplan asked, and Carstairs nodded his head while he adjusted his glasses. "Tell me, Mr. Carstairs, do you think he'd tell you if he was in trouble?"

"I happen to be an experienced certified public accountant. I intend to do a thorough review of the firm's books, which will tell me exactly how serious the firm's capital situation is at the moment and what the prospects are. As for what Eli Strauss might tell me, frankly, I hadn't planned on asking him anything. That's why I arranged for Mr. Guttman to accompany me."

"It sounds great," Miss Brady said. "At least we'll be able to know how that end of things stand. Incidentally, what's the rest of the story on Mrs. Cole?"

"You'll have to ask Mr. Guttman," Dora Kaplan said quickly.

"Wasn't you there?" Mishkin asked.

"Sure I was there, but only Guttman knows what's going on."

"Mrs. Kaplan and I talked to the nephew's wife," Guttman said as they turned to him. "She didn't see Cohen that day, but she said her husband seen him at his office. Also, Mrs. Cole mentioned something about Cohen's insurance, which is what I already asked Miss Brady to check."

"Well, with Cohen already signing over everything else to the Center, the insurance is about all we have to go on," Miss Brady said.

"What you're saying is maybe they was so worried about getting the money, they killed Cohen before he could get married to Miss Walters and make the insurance to her?" Mishkin suggested.

"Well, we got to figure, Cohen was an old man and he wasn't healthy," Guttman explained. "So the thing is, if somebody killed him, it had to be in a hurry, otherwise they could've just waited until he died natural."

"There's still the question of the will," Mrs. Kaplan said. "We don't know how much he left to the nephew, or didn't leave to him."

"The important thing maybe isn't the will at all," Guttman corrected. "What matters is if the nephew thought he was getting nothing, and from what his wife said yesterday, that's what I think."

"You said that Mrs. Cole hadn't seen Cohen for a while," Mrs. O'Rourke said. "Does that mean she couldn't have had anything to do with his demise?"

Demise, Guttman thought. Where does everybody get these words?

"It don't say anything about the husband, though," Mishkin offered.

"I think I should tell you all that yesterday Mr. Guttman practically told Mrs. Cole that we were investigating Mr. Cohen's death," Dora Kaplan said.

They were silent for a moment, each looking at Guttman, then at one another. Finally, Mr. Carstairs spoke. "I thought we weren't going to do anything like that," he said.

"It wasn't like I wanted to," Guttman said. "But the way it was turning out, I decided the only thing was to see what kind of a reaction it got with her."

"And?" Miss Brady prompted.

"And it was very interesting. Also, I figured she was gonna tell her husband about the visit, and as soon as we showed up to talk to him, he'd know something was up. So this way, he'll have more time to worry, if he's got something to hide."

"And more time to prepare a good story for you," Mrs. O'Rourke said.

"That could also be," Guttman admitted. "But when a person's got lots of time to think up lies, they always get them too complicated, they always say too much."

"You know this from being a detective?" Mrs. Kaplan asked.

"I know this from being a person," Guttman told her. "It happens to me, if I decide not to tell somebody the truth, that the best thing is to say as little as I can. But the more time I got to think about it, the more I get myself in trouble."

"That's an interesting philosophy, Mr. Guttman," Carstairs said.

"Sounds like me," Margaret Brady added.

"I'd like to go back to my room for a moment, and then I think we should get started downtown for our appointment, Mr. Guttman," Carstairs said.

Guttman glanced at his watch. "I'll meet you here," he said, glad that he'd decided to wear a sport jacket instead of his usual sweater.

"Well, I'd better go see what I can do about getting another

110

look at the records," Miss Brady said. "It's easier if I wait until someone goes to the ladies' room than if I try to sneak in at night. This way I feel less like a burglar."

"What would you have the rest of us do?" Mrs. O'Rourke asked.

"Well, since too many people going to see the partner wouldn't work so well, I guess there isn't anything for now," Guttman said.

"It seems to me that we really haven't had very much to do from the start," Mrs. O'Rourke said, surprising Guttman.

"So what do you want to do?" Mishkin asked.

"We're supposed to be investigating a murder, aren't we? So why don't we investigate?"

"Who's stopping you?" Mishkin asked.

"No one is telling me what to do," Mrs. O'Rourke replied.

"Okay," Guttman said with a small sigh. "So tell me, what kind investigating you got in mind?"

"Well, we should be out questioning people, checking up on our suspects," Mrs. O'Rourke said hesitantly.

"We can't all go at once," Guttman told her. "And right now we got only two possible suspects. We got the nephew and the partner."

"You're forgetting your friend Mr. Carstairs," Mrs. Kaplan said.

"I'm not forgetting," Guttman said, although he knew that he wasn't considering Carstairs as a suspect. "The thing is, it ain't like you didn't contribute nothing, Mrs. O'Rourke. After all, who was it learned about the Bowseniors, what told us about Cohen fighting with his nephew? And who found out about Mr. Carstairs?" He looked quickly behind him to make sure that Carstairs hadn't returned. "I tell you what, how about if you talk to the people here again, maybe there's some you missed. We might learn something else that could help."

"That's right," Mrs. O'Rourke said. "On television the witnesses often remember something important that they forgot at first."

"So it's worth a try," Guttman said.

"I think I'll have a talk with my Phyllis tonight," Mrs. Kaplan said slowly. "Maybe we can find out a little more about the Coles."

"It would be good to know if maybe they need money," Guttman suggested. "Meanwhile, I guess I better get ready to go with Carstairs. When I get back I'll tell you what happened." Then he got up and went to the men's room, before meeting Carstairs at the front door.

"We'll have to take a taxi," Carstairs said as they went outside. "I phoned for one from my room."

"A taxi?"

"There isn't enough time for the bus," Carstairs explained. "We don't want to be late."

"Naturally," Guttman said, trying to remember how much money he had in his wallet. Usually he didn't carry more than ten or fifteen dollars, and he hoped he had enough to pay for his share of the fare. He didn't have to worry. After the twenty-five-minute trip Carstairs insisted on paying, explaining that it would be paid for eventually by his old company, since he really was going to review the books for Fancy Fair, and the accountants would be paid as part of their regular fee.

Fancy Fair wasn't in the heart of a garment district like the one Guttman had known for so many years. It wasn't crowded with men pushing carts and racks laden with heavy rolls of cloth and garments, trucks double-parked everywhere. Even the buildings were different; they weren't as high. Of course, Guttman thought, just about all kinds of buildings is different, here. Fancy Fair was on the second floor of a six-story building. When the elevator doors opened they were in a large, well-furnished reception area, with a large desk for the receptionist. On the walls were sketches and photographs of the lines that Fancy Fair produced. While Carstairs talked to the girl, Guttman studied the designs critically. Middle-line, he thought. Not too expensive, not too cheap. But not with special original designs. Take someone's design, make a few changes, and you got a line of your own. Not a steal-and-sell business, but not high-fashion, either.

Guttman, in his years in the garment business, had worked almost exclusively for middle-line manufacturers. It was, he had learned, a bit more stable than other segments of the industry. And a good cutter, who could get the most out of every bolt of cloth, was highly appreciated.

"We're expected," Carstairs said to him.

Guttman took a last look at the pictures and followed Carstairs through a door to the shop. Eli Strauss had an office in the working area, with metal and glass partitions that allowed him to see what was going on but kept most of the noise out. It was a good-sized office, with a cluttered desk, a couch, several chairs for visitors and a drawing board. There were sketches and swatches of fabric pinned to a bulletin board that filled the wall opposite the shop.

"Harold, it's nice to see you again," Eli Strauss said, getting up from behind his desk.

"Eli, this is Mr. Guttman."

"How do you do?"

"It's a pleasure," Guttman answered, shaking his hand.

Eli Strauss was in his late fifties, perhaps early sixties, medium-height and stockily built. He was working in his shirt sleeves, with his tie loose and his collar unbuttoned. Strauss had a square face and a jutting nose that seemed to stand out even more because he had only a tiny fringe of hair around his ears.

"So what can I do for you, Harold?" he asked, settling down behind the desk.

"I'm in to take a look at the books, that's all. I thought I should drop in and say hello," Carstairs answered.

"We just had that kid, what's his name, in a couple of weeks ago," Strauss said.

"You might call this a checkup," Carstairs explained. "Fred is one of our bright young men, and they're thinking about moving him up soon, but they wanted to, well, make sure. Since

114

I used to do your books, they asked me if I'd mind taking a peek. You don't mind, I hope."

"Of course not," Strauss said. "But I thought you were retired."

"I am. But I suppose I just like to keep my hand in. The firm has always been very important to me, you know."

"Yeah, Sam used to keep coming in here, too," Strauss said. "Couldn't stay away. First he couldn't wait to retire and then he couldn't stay away."

"I couldn't handle any of the clients on a regular basis," Carstairs said. "Frankly, I suppose I'm too old for that sort of regular grind. But since I'm familiar with Fancy Free . . ."

"You'd better be, after the way you juggled the books for all those years," Strauss interrupted, smiling.

"As you say." Carstairs returned the smile.

"They pay you for this?"

"Not directly," Carstairs said.

"You mean it's off the books, huh?" Strauss laughed. "No taxes to pay, no problems with social security—oh, you accountants . . ."

Carstairs looked embarrassed, but he managed a smile. Guttman wondered whether Strauss was right, or if Carstairs was only acting. He knew better than to ask, though. The phone rang, and while Strauss was busy, Guttman stared out the glass wall at the shop. Smaller than some he had worked in, but not much. But no matter what the size was, somehow they were always the same. After a moment he located the cutters—three of them, two who were probably Mexican and an older man. He's probably not much younger than me, Guttman thought.

"Okay," Strauss said, hanging up the phone. "So you want to spend some time with the books. Tell Gertrude what you want, she'll get it for you. You know Gertrude, right?"

"Of course."

"Fine. What else, Harold?"

"Else?"

"Your friend here, Mr. Guttman. He's not an accountant too, is he?"

"No . . ."

"And he's not just along for the ride, either," Strauss said.

"Mr. Strauss . . ." Guttman began.

"Call me Eli. And you're . . . ?"

"Max Guttman."

"Okay, Max. Now, what's this all about?"

"Well, it's a little awkward . . ."

Strauss looked at Carstairs quickly, and raised an eyebrow.

"It's about your partner, Cohen," Guttman said.

"What about him?"

"Well, the first thing I should say is that I know what I'm gonna ask is none of my business."

"I figured that out, too," Strauss said, smiling. "But if Harold brought you, I'll talk to you. I have to," he joked. "If I don't, with what Harold knows about this business, all he's got to do is talk to my competitors and I'm ruined."

"I appreciate your cooperation," Guttman said. "The thing is, like I said, it's about your partner, Mr. Cohen . . ."

"Wait a minute," Strauss interrupted. "Don't tell me. It's that nutty old woman again, right? The one who kept calling up all the time?"

"Not exactly . . ."

"That means yes."

"She's dead," Guttman said quietly.

"Oh . . ."

"She was very upset by what happened with Mr. Cohen. She got into a depression, and she died," he explained.

"I'm sorry to hear about it," Strauss said. "I didn't know her, but if Cohen was planning on marrying her, well, I would have figured she was all right. Until she started with those phone calls."

"What did she say when she made the calls?" Guttman asked.

"As near as I could figure it, she was telling me that I killed Sam."

"She said that?"

"More or less. She said, 'You killed him, you all killed him.'"

"Do you know what she meant by that?"

"No, not really," Strauss said. "Then, when I thought about it, I figured maybe she had some idea that I was asking him to help out in the business, you know, and that wasn't the best thing for Sam, in his condition. But even that didn't really make sense."

"You mean you didn't ask him?"

"I didn't ask him, and aside from stopping in to chew the fat every week or two, Sam didn't do anything around here after he finally retired."

"You said before he couldn't stay away," Guttman reminded him.

"That's right. Like I said, once a week or so. But just to talk, maybe it gave him something to do, I don't know."

"Would you've wanted Cohen to help?"

"Look, Max . . ." Strauss leaned forward with his forearms on the desk. "Sam and I were partners for twenty years. After that much time together, you either hate somebody or you kind of love him. I didn't hate Sam. I don't know, maybe I didn't love him, either. But I sure as hell wouldn't ask him to do anything to endanger his health. Hell, I was the one who talked him into retiring in the first place." Strauss shook his head. "Look, Max, when Sam retired, it hurt the business. He more than held up his end of things, believe me. But this isn't the easiest way in the world to make a living, the pressures . . . Ah . . ." Strauss sighed.

"In New York, I was a cutter," Guttman said. "Until I retired."

"Okay, then. So you know." Strauss took a cigarette from the pack on his desk.

"Do you suppose there could've been somebody else making aggravation for him?" Guttman asked.

"Like who?"

"I'm asking, Mr. Strauss. I'm not telling."

"I don't know. I guess the old woman thought so . . ." Strauss stopped to think for a moment. "Look, this doesn't make any sense."

"Maybe you could tell us, anyway," Guttman prompted.

"I'm not even sure why you're asking. I know I said I'd talk to you because Harold brought you, but . . ."

"Mr. Strauss, there's lots of people at the Center what's upset by all this. Some of them believed what Miss Walters was saying, and that worries them a lot."

"So why keep asking questions about it?" Strauss asked. "Why not just forget it and let it die down?"

"Some things take a long time to forget, and let's face it, some of these people ain't got maybe so long. Besides, it's better if they know for sure in their minds, one way or the other."

Strauss looked at Guttman for a moment, his brow furrowed. "All right," he said. "After what you just said, I probably shouldn't be telling you this . . ." He lit his cigarette, finally. "When the old lady called, Miss Walters, sometimes it was for me, sometimes it was for Larry."

"Larry?"

"Larry Cole. He's Sam's nephew. And I don't know what Sam might have told her, but Larry wasn't too keen on having Sam retire. Maybe it was his wife's fault. She was afraid if Sam retired, he'd just hang around the house all day with her, I guess. I don't know. Anyway, the old lady kept calling, and I finally called the Center, that doctor, what's his name . . ."

"Dr. Morton," Carstairs said.

"Yeah. Anyway, I told him about it and said if he couldn't stop the calls, he should take the phone out of her room, or something."

"The calls bothered you so much?" Guttman asked.

"Not me," Strauss said. "I mean, sure, I didn't like it, but it was Rita, she's the girl on the board. After a while Larry and I both told her not to put the calls through, and one day she walks in here with tears in her eyes and says if I don't get that woman to stop, she'll quit. So I called the doctor."

"Mr. Strauss, you been very helpful," Guttman said. "Incidentally, I didn't know the nephew worked here."

"He's a salesman. Not the best in the world, but not the worst, either. He's learning."

"Uh huh," Guttman said. "What I was wondering, what

would you say if I asked you, do you think what Miss Walters told could be the truth?"

"You mean that someone—me, or Larry—killed Sam?"

"Let's say someone."

"They told me he died of a heart attack," Strauss said, his face impassive. "Nobody's told me otherwise, except that Miss Walters. And she was out of her mind."

"You don't believe it, then."

"No reason to believe it."

"Miss Walters believed it, until she died," Guttman said.

"Well, I won't believe it, until I die," Strauss said. Then he smiled. "And I hope that's not for a little while yet."

The phone rang again, and Strauss reached to answer it. Guttman was aware that Carstairs was looking at him a little uneasily, but he pretended not to notice.

"I want to thank you again," Guttman said as soon as Strauss hung up the phone. "I was wondering, by the way, was Cohen still a partner here, even if he was retired?"

"Sure. He wasn't drawing a salary, but he still had his piece of the business."

"That's what somebody told me," Guttman said. "Did you know that when somebody decides to live in the Center permanent, they sign a paper giving everything to the home after they die?"

"Yeah," Strauss said. "Sam and I talked about it."

"And?"

"And nothing. It wasn't really resolved. I couldn't buy out his interest, not now, anyway, and he had to make his own decisions about what he wanted to sign over, and so forth."

"Couldn't you work something out to have the corporation buy up his interest, perhaps get a note from the bank?" Carstairs suggested.

"We tried. But the way business has been . . ." Strauss sighed.

"So now the Center owns the business?" Guttman asked.

"Sam's share only," Strauss said quickly. "Yeah, I guess so."

"Is that going to mean problems for you?"

"I don't see why. Unless someone over there tries to tell me how to run a garment house." Strauss eased back in his chair and looked first at Carstairs, then at Guttman. "Anything else?" he asked.

"Just to thank you," Guttman said.

"Okay. I've got something, then. I'm not dumb, and I've got a pretty good idea of why you're asking all these questions. Now, so far as I'm concerned, you're out of your mind. I mean, I figure Sam had a heart attack. It's a weakness of mine, believing in doctors. But after that business with the old lady, I figured I'd let you ask your questions and give you the answers, and that would be the end of it. I hope I'm right."

"I'm sorry if it was a bother to you," Guttman said.

"It's okay," Strauss answered. "Just so long as we understand each other. And, Harold"—he turned to Carstairs—"suppose I called Mike Bushman and asked him whether he knows you're here. What would he say?"

"Just what I told you, Eli," Carstairs said. "That's the reason I'm here. To check to make sure that Fred's as good as they think he is. However, if you'd rather I didn't look at the books, or if you'd like to call Mr. Bushman, go right ahead. I'll understand."

"Nah, never mind," Strauss said. "Go ahead and look all you like. That it, then?"

"That's it, and thank you," Guttman said.

"I'm sorry we took so much of your time, Eli," Carstairs said.

On the way out Guttman stopped at the reception desk and asked about Mr. Cole. The girl said he'd gone to lunch but should be back in about an hour. Guttman told her he'd be back.

Carstairs led Guttman to a small cafeteria, where they had lunch. "The food is plain," he explained, "but it's clean here. And it's nice not to be hurried while you eat." They sat at a table for four, and while they were there two men joined them, separately, to eat and depart. Like at the Automat in New York, Guttman thought. Except, of course, no putting coins in the slots.

"You didn't ask Eli anything about the insurance," Carstairs said.

"I thought about it, but I decided you'd find out when you looked the books over. And something like that, it would be better if he didn't know we found out."

"I expect so," Carstairs said. "Do you have any opinion, so far?"

"About Strauss?" Guttman asked. "Well, I'd say he seems like a nice man. Probably a good boss, too. Not easy, but fair."

After lunch they returned to Fancy Fair. Carstairs went off to the bookkeeper's office, and Guttman sat down in the reception room to await the return of Lawrence Cole. It turned out to be a long wait.

Lawrence Cole's office was more expensively furnished than Eli Strauss'. The floor was carpeted with a beige shag, while the walls were paneled with a dark wood. The couch and chairs were leather, adding to the impression of richness and solidarity. Against one wall was an elaborate bar, with shelves of glasses behind it and a number of bottles. The only pictures on the walls, however, were of dress designs, and there were enough papers on the large desk to make it look like a real working office. Well, Guttman thought, he's a salesman, and a salesman has to impress people sometimes. He wondered whether this had once been Samuel Cohen's office.

Cole was standing behind his desk, waiting for Guttman. He was well over six feet tall, and broad, with only a hint of approaching middle-age spread. Guttman felt slightly uncomfortable when Cole didn't offer to shake hands, and he waited until Cole indicated that he should sit down. Guttman pushed the chair back several inches further from the desk so he'd have enough leg room. Cole was two or three inches taller than Guttman, and the old man wasn't used to looking up at people. As a young man he'd towered above most people. Now people seemed to grow taller.

"I want to thank you for—" Guttman began, but Cole interrupted.

"Let's get something straight right off. The only reason I decided to see you was to tell you to stop bothering me."

"Bothering you?" Guttman said. "This is the first time I ever seen you."

"You saw my wife yesterday," Cole said.

He was a handsome man, Guttman thought, but there was something about his mouth that made him look almost as though he was going to cry if he didn't get something he wanted.

"I don't know what this is all about," Cole went on. "But I want it stopped."

"Mr. Cole, I'm sorry if I'm upsetting you . . ."

"You upset my wife. First that crazy old woman with her phone calls, now you."

It was the third, perhaps the fourth, time that Guttman had heard about the "crazy old woman," and suddenly it angered him. "Look, you don't want to talk to me, you just say so and I'll go out the door," he said sharply. "You said you'd talk to me, so okay. Otherwise, I'm leaving now."

"And you'll go on pestering me, right?" Cole asked, but his tone was a bit milder.

"Mr. Cole, I started out to say I was going to thank you for talking to me. I know you don't have to, and I appreciate if you would," Guttman said, letting his own anger fade. "But," he added, "I don't have to get yelled on, either."

"All right," Cole said, sitting down behind his desk. "Let's get it over with."

"The first thing, then, is that you're right," Guttman said. "It is partly because of Miss Walters that I'm coming here."

"I suppose I should be grateful that you didn't start calling my home at all hours of the night."

"I got nothing to do with what Miss Walters done . . ."

"Wild accusations, practically threatening my wife . . ."

"Miss Walters made threats?"

" 'God will punish the evil and the wicked,' " Cole quoted. "Something like that. The phone would ring, maybe ten o'clock, maybe two in the morning, and when you pick it up there's a nut telling you God will punish the wicked."

"I knew she made some phone calls," Guttman said. "But nobody said nothing about threats like that." He wasn't sure that he believed Cole, but he decided not to make an issue of it.

"Well, if you had nothing to do with it, don't worry about it. Now, what brings you here? Why did you go see my wife?"

"It's about your uncle," Guttman said. "I wonder, could I ask you—"

"Forget it," Cole said, shaking his head. "For a while I figured okay, let the old man come in and talk, let him get it off his chest, be a nice guy, humor him and he'll go away, but—"

"I didn't ask you should humor me. I just ask would you answer some questions about your uncle."

"What was between me and my uncle is none of your damn business. I've got nothing more to say to you, except you'd damn well better not bother my wife again. Is that clear?"

Guttman looked at him for a moment, then nodded his head and stood up. "It's very clear. Some of us old people, even if you got to humor us, we can still hear. We could understand. Some of us could even think, like other human beings." He walked to the door, then turned to look at Cole again. "I'm sorry I disturbed you so much. I'm even more sorry it was such a waste of my time."

Guttman thought about slamming the door behind him, but decided that would be childish, and it was bad enough that people were treating him like a child without him acting that way. It would be a nice thing, he thought, if this Cole was the one what killed his uncle. It would give me pleasure to find out.

He found Mr. Carstairs in the bookkeeper's office, sitting at a long table with ledgers and books spread out in front of him. Carstairs seemed to be enjoying himself.

"How did it go?" he asked.

"I'll tell you later." Guttman looked at the collection of papers in front of Carstairs. "You gonna be long?"

"Most of the rest of the afternoon, I expect."

"Okay. So I'll go back alone."

"If I don't see you later this afternoon, we'll talk in the morning," Carstairs said, glancing at the bookkeeper.

"Okay," Guttman agreed. "Have a nice afternoon."

He had to take a cab back to the Center. They'd used a taxi coming in, and Guttman didn't know which bus would take him back. He found a cab line a block away from Fancy Fair's offices, and leaned in the window of the first in the line to ask how much it would cost to get him back.

"About four and a half, maybe five bucks, Pop," the driver told him. "Plus tip."

It would take most of his pocket money for the week, but he knew without looking that he had enough in his wallet to cover it. He got in and gave the driver the address, wishing he remembered how much Carstairs had paid on the way in so he'd know whether he was being cheated.

Feeling a little like a sneak thief, Guttman went into the library when he got back. He wanted some time to be alone to think, and he didn't want to talk to Mrs. Kaplan or Mrs. O'Rourke just yet. Unfortunately, the Bowseniors were in the library. Hoping that they hadn't seen him, Guttman backed out.

For a moment he thought about sitting outside, but it was getting a little cooler, and he thought his cold might be getting worse. Okay, he thought, so I'll get a cup of tea and sit in the snack lounge. This morning they was complaining about not knowing what was going on, so now I'll tell them.

Surprisingly, Mishkin was alone at the table, playing solitaire as usual. Guttman got his tea and went to join him.

"Where is everybody?" he asked.

"Brady, I don't know. Kaplan and O'Rourke, they went painting again. Sit down, we'll play some pinochle. How did it go?"

Guttman shrugged. "I left Carstairs there. He was busy with the bookkeeping stuff."

"Did anything happen?" Mishkin asked, dealing the cards.

"I talked to the partner. He seems like a nice person, but he didn't really tell me nothing. The nephew, that one I could do without, thank you."

"He was there, too?"

"He works there," Guttman said. "A real no-goodnik."

"Nu, so who says you got to like a suspect?" Mishkin asked.

"Nobody. In fact, it's better if you don't like," Guttman said. "That way you can hope he done it. You know, it was funny, the way Carstairs was there. He seemed different. I guess he was a pretty big accountant, you know, not just a bookkeeper. For big companies, too."

"So what's funny if he's different there?" Mishkin asked. "Everybody's different when they're where they belong. A man goes to work, he's something. Here," he said, looking around, "here it's different. Here, nobody is somebody."

"Everybody is somebody," Guttman said.

"Of course, but there's a difference."

"I guess."

"With the women," Mishkin went on, playing his cards carefully, "it's different."

"Why should it be so different for them?"

"Because for them it's gradual. The kids grow up, they don't need so much attention, little by little there's less for them to do. With a man, it happens all at once. One day he's working, the next day he's not."

"At the beginning it's nice," Guttman said, remembering when he had retired.

"Like a vacation," Mishkin agreed. "It's only when you finally figure out you're not gonna do anything the rest of your life, that's when it's a problem."

"It don't seem to bother you so much," Guttman said.

"I don't think about it."

"You don't think about it, how come you just talked about it like that?"

"Okay," Mishkin conceded. "So I try not to think about it. I take things one at a time. I don't think about tomorrow when I could help it, and I remember yesterday only when I'm alone, like in my room."

"I never asked, Mishkin. You got a family?"

"I got three sons and a daughter. My wife died maybe fifteen years ago. I got a son in San Francisco, one in Washington, another son in San Diego, and the daughter lives in New York. They're all married, they all got children. Upstairs, in my room, I got so many pictures of grandchildren, there's hardly room on the dresser. Some I never seen, even."

"It's none of my business, but you decided to stay here instead of with them?" Guttman asked.

"I thought about it," Mishkin said. "You're lucky, Guttman. You got a daughter you get along with, so you live there. You got only one kid."

"A son died in the war," Guttman told him.

"I still got all of mine. But . . ." He shrugged. "There's too many, you see. If I stay with only one, they're good children, they say Poppa, come stay with us too. Maybe they feel guilty, maybe they got together and decide I should spend three months with each, I don't know. But running around that way, one to the other, it's no good. They talked me into retiring, come spend time with us, they said. And they meant it," Mishkin said. "But," he sighed, "it was a mistake. I was always visiting, always a guest. I was never there long enough, anyplace, to belong. So I came here, finally."

They played out the hand in silence, and then, as Guttman took his turn shuffling the cards, Mishkin went on as if he hadn't stopped at all.

"I get letters, I get phone calls. It's not like they don't care. But visits, that's something else. It's hard for them. My son in San Diego, he comes up here on business sometimes, maybe once a month, and when he does, he always makes sure he's got at least a couple of hours to visit. Even if he's got to take a plane at midnight, or the next morning, when he's here, he comes to see me. My son in San Francisco, if they go on vacation, if they drive this way, they always stop. But how long could they stay? What kind of vacation is it for the children to visit me here for a couple of hours?"

They finished playing the hand of pinochle. Guttman won, knowing that Mishkin wasn't really concentrating.

"They're all different ages," Mishkin said. "That's probably why there ain't too much closeness between them. There's twenty years between the oldest and the youngest. The oldest, he's the one visits from San Diego. You know, that's the part that bothers me the most, when I think about it. They're not so close to each other. They call each other for birthdays, they send cards. But they're not so close to each other . . ."

They concentrated on playing cards after that, until they were finally joined by Mrs. Kaplan and Mrs. O'Rourke, fresh

126

from their painting class. While the entire group wasn't there, Guttman decided to tell them about his trip downtown, anyway. That way they wouldn't complain.

Guttman almost didn't make it the next morning. Lois caught him sniffling, and immediately demanded that he go to bed while she tried to find a doctor. It took twenty minutes of debate, during which Lois extracted a promise that he'd see the doctors at the Center, before she agreed to let him go. When he arrived, Guttman went straight to the snack lounge. At the moment he was more interested in a cup of tea than he was in a visit to the doctor. That could wait for a while.

"I see everybody's here," Guttman said.

"Everybody but your friend Mr. Carstairs," Mrs. O'Rourke pointed out.

"So we'll wait a couple of minutes," Guttman said, stirring sugar into his tea and wondering just how to go about making an appointment to be examined by one of the doctors. Mr. Carstairs arrived before he got around to asking anyone about it.

"Okay," Guttman said. "So now everybody is here and we can begin. Since we was waiting for you, why don't you be the first, Mr. Carstairs? What did you learn yesterday?"

"As you suspected, Mr. Guttman, there were records regarding the insurance that Mr. Strauss and Mr. Cohen had. In the event of the death of either of them, fifty thousand dollars was to be paid."

"Who got the money?"

"The policy was payable to the company."

"That's a lot of money," Mrs. O'Rourke said.

"People have killed for less than that," Mrs. Kaplan added.

"And the money, with Strauss being the only partner, it's the same as if it went to him, no?" Guttman asked.

"Not really," Carstairs explained. "If it were payable to Mr. Strauss, then he'd be free to do with the insurance money as he pleased. As it happens, the money is added to the firm's capital."

"And he isn't the firm by himself, right?" Mishkin asked.

"That's right," Carstairs said. "He owns only fifty percent of the business."

"So who owns the rest?" Mrs. Kaplan asked.

"Golden Valley owns forty percent," Miss Brady said. "At least, that's how much Cohen turned over to them when he signed his residence agreement."

"And Lawrence Cole holds the other ten percent," Carstairs said.

"Well, where does that leave us?" Agnes O'Rourke asked.

"It leaves us knowing what we already figured out," Guttman said. "Except now we got details."

"I don't think I understand," Mrs. O'Rourke complained.

"Well, we knew from what he said that Strauss knew Cohen was signing over the business. And we also knew that the nephew knew about it, because he wasn't happy about the whole thing, including the marriage plans with Miss Walters."

"Then it doesn't help, does it?"

"It might," Margaret Brady said. "Didn't someone mention something about this firm, this Fancy whatever, not being in the best of shape?"

"The financial condition could have been better," Carstairs agreed.

"Then this fifty thousand couldn't have hurt," she said.

"No, as a matter of fact, it might have been considered a windfall for the business," Carstairs said.

"And if you got a business with new partners coming in," Mishkin said, "it wouldn't hurt if your business wasn't in money trouble."

"It looks like we got another suspect," Dora Kaplan said. "The partner could have had a reason, after all."

"Don't forget the nephew, either," Guttman said. "We still don't know for sure that he knew Cohen already signed everything over."

"For that matter, we don't know that this partner, Strauss, wasn't aware that the papers had been signed," Mishkin added.

"Let me offer another thought," Margaret Brady said quietly. "When I first brought up the question of these residence agreements, I had something in mind. The Center isn't in the best of financial shape. And Dr. Morton has some very ambitious plans, but he won't be able to do anything about them unless things settle down."

"I thought there was a board of directors," Guttman said.

"That's right, but as administrator of the Center, Dr. Morton has the responsibility for making this a paying operation."

"So Cohen dying and the Center getting the interest in the business wouldn't hurt that way, either," Guttman said.

"You don't suspect Dr. Morton, do you?" Mrs. O'Rourke asked.

"I'm just raising the question," Miss Brady answered.

It was a question they didn't really want to think about, though. The Golden Valley Irregulars sat silently for a moment, avoiding each other's gaze. Then Mrs. Kaplan spoke.

"I've got a little extra information," she said. "About the nephew. You remember that I told you my Phyllis knows them? Well, I asked her about it, and it seems that the Coles aren't really that well off."

"That's a nice house they live in," Guttman said.

"Exactly. Only it was paid for by Cohen. Most of it, anyway. And he used to live there with them," Dora Kaplan said.

"You mean it was his house?"

"No, he gave it to them, but it was on condition that he could live there as long as he liked," Mrs. Kaplan told him.

"Well, I guess it's interesting, but so what?" Miss Brady asked. "I mean, what do we do with that?"

"I don't know what anybody else does with it, but me, I'm gonna go find a doctor about my cold. And then I'm gonna do some thinking. There's something in all this that don't make sense, and I'm only hoping I can figure it out," Guttman told them.

"If you tell us what's bothering you, maybe we could help," Mrs. Kaplan suggested.

"If I knew what it was, I'd be glad to tell you. Only I don't." They looked disappointed when Guttman got up from the table, but there was nothing he could do about it. At least not now.

The nurse told him that it was a little irregular, but if he'd wait, she'd check with Dr. Morton and see whether he'd see Guttman. Clinic was usually held at nine-thirty, and here it was ten-thirty already. Guttman thanked her and sat down to wait, until she ushered him into the doctor's office.

"Mr. Guttman, this is a surprise," Dr. Morton said, getting up from his chair.

"A surprise?"

"Yes. I was going to see whether you could stop by to see me later this morning."

"But you didn't know I had a cold," Guttman said.

"No, but I'm glad you came to see me about that. You know, we have to be very careful around here."

"It's just a little cold."

"Can't be too careful," the doctor said. "You can never tell about complications. Let's take a look at you," he suggested, putting a thermometer in Guttman's mouth. He took a stethoscope from the pocket of his white jacket and listened to Guttman's breathing. Then he checked the thermometer.

"Well, no fever, really."

"You mean there's a little?"

"Ninety-nine point two. Not enough to worry about. How do you feel?"

"I feel like I got a cold, that's all," Guttman said. "I sniffle a little, my head feels a little stuffed, that's all."

"Open your mouth." Guttman did as he was told. "Looks all right," Dr. Morton said, dropping the wooden tongue depressor in the wastebasket. "I don't think there's anything to worry about, but I'll give you a prescription, anyway. Doesn't hurt to play it safe. Forgive me," he added, "but with a man of your age, well . . ."

"Oh, sure," Guttman said. "I understand."

"Good. You know, a cold is one thing, but if it's a touch of the flu, well, I'm glad you came in to see me. It's always best to check."

"Uh huh," Guttman said, watching him write the prescription. He decided to wait to ask about the bocce courts. First he'd see what Mr. Bowsenior had to say. Maybe the residents' council had met.

"You can get this filled at the pharmacy, just down the hall. No charge."

"I appreciate that."

"Not at all. It's all part of the membership," Dr. Morton said.

"I didn't realize," Guttman told him. "But the drugs, they cost money, don't they?"

"Medicaire," the doctor explained. "The finest thing this nation ever did for its senior citizens."

"It's very good. Well, thank you," Guttman said, getting up.

"Uh, Mr. Guttman, if you wouldn't mind waiting a moment . . ."

Guttman sat down. "Something's wrong?" he asked.

"Well, yes, in a manner of speaking. This is a bit awkward, but the fact of the matter is, I've received a phone call about you . . ."

"Ah," Guttman said. "Don't tell me, I could guess. Cole?"

"Well, that isn't really the point, after all—"

"Don't worry about it," Guttman interrupted. "I'm not bothering him any more. I'm sorry he called you and made a fuss, but you don't have to worry."

"Well, I'm certainly not worried, Mr. Guttman, but I do have the reputation of the Center to think about, and after that unfortunate business with Miss Walters, well . . ."

"Look, believe me, nothing happened," Guttman said.

"Mr. Cole said you went to see his wife, and that you upset her rather badly."

"Mr. Cole said that, huh? Well, Mr. Cole is lying. If you don't believe me, go ask Mrs. Kaplan. She was there."

"I don't think that's really the point, Mr. Guttman," Dr.

Morton said slowly. "But I would like to know what this is all about." He picked up a pipe from the ashtray on his desk and began filling it.

"Well, it's kind of hard knowing where to begin . . ."

"Let me see if I can help you. From what Mr. Cole said, I have the impression that you're still . . . concerned about poor Miss Walters. Is that it?"

"Sort of," Guttman admitted.

"And now you've taken it upon yourself to conduct an investigation, haven't you?"

"I don't know if you'd call it an investigation, but . . ."

"Mr. Guttman, do you honestly believe that there is anything to what Miss Walters was saying?" Dr. Morton asked, leaning forward in his chair. "Do you really suppose that, well, I don't know, that someone killed Samuel Cohen?"

Guttman looked at him for a moment, then sighed. "To be completely honest, I don't know what I believe. No, that isn't true. I know, but I can't say it."

"Why not?"

"Because it isn't sure yet. The main thing is," Guttman explained, "some of the people was upset by all this. So they asked me if I could check things out, that's all."

"And you did?"

"I did what I could."

"But you haven't found anything to bear out their suspicions?" Dr. Morton asked.

"I wouldn't even call it suspicions. More it was a worry that maybe . . . you know?"

"Yes, I suppose so," the doctor said with a sigh.

"Anyway, I tried to find out. Cohen was a rich man, maybe somebody wanted his money. This Cole, his nephew, is not a nice person. People do a lot of things for money, and Cohen was rich, like I said. Then there was a partner, and who knows what's really between partners in a business? Someone even told me about Mr. Carstairs . . ."

"Mr. Carstairs?"

"Harold Carstairs. He lives here. He used to be an accountant."

"Oh, yes. Of course. What about him?"

"Well, he was in love with Miss Walters, so somebody said what if he was so jealous, maybe he done something to Cohen."

"I find that a little far-fetched," Dr. Morton said.

"Far, near, it don't matter. What counts is people was worried about things like this. So I looked into things."

"But you found nothing," the doctor repeated.

"I wouldn't say nothing. I found out lots of things. I found out who bought the home this Cole got. I found out how Cohen's partner didn't have enough money to buy his shares when Cohen retired. I found out how the company wasn't in such good shape, but the insurance from Cohen dying would probably help a little. I found out about how Cohen made his insurance to Miss Walters instead of the nephew and how he was so upset he wanted to get Cohen declared incompetent or something. And I found out how Carstairs keeps acting like everything's normal, only somehow it don't seem right. Except he don't believe anything happened."

"Well," Dr. Morton said after a moment, "that's quite a bit of research you've done. But what does it all mean?"

"I ain't exactly decided what it means, yet."

"I see." The doctor finally lit his pipe. It smelled as bad as one of Guttman's cigars. "Mr. Guttman, unless you have found something that could be considered evidence of a crime, I'm going to have to ask you to give up this little . . . escapade. And if you have found something that could be considered evidence, then I suggest you go to the police with it."

"Doctor, the thing is—"

"Mr. Guttman, I'm responsible for this Center. I'm responsible for everyone here at Golden Valley. I simply can't have our people going around poking their noses into other people's personal lives like this. Besides," he added more gently, "it really isn't good for our people. There's no reason for them getting upset by something like this."

"Dr. Morton, I agree with you. There's just one thing I want you should know. I didn't have this idea in the first place. And also, I made sure everybody didn't find out things they could talk about that could upset anybody else."

134

"I'm sure that's so, Mr. Guttman. But still, I have to ask you to end this . . . investigation."

"I understand," Guttman said, getting up. "Thank you again for the prescription."

"I hope I didn't sound too harsh," Dr. Morton said. "But something like this, well . . ."

"I know you're only trying to help."

"I appreciate your cooperation."

When he was through at the pharmacy Guttman went to the library, where he was able to sit by himself and think. Dr. Morton had told him to stop the whole thing, and if he was being honest with himself, Guttman didn't really mind. After all, done is done, and beating on a dead horse with a stick is only gonna make you tired, he thought. Talking to people, looking into their lives, and the whole big deal is that some people could've needed money. So that's a reason to say Cohen was killed? We started at the wrong place, he thought. What we should've done was start with trying to prove something happened, and then we could've let the police do the work. Or even if we did the questioning by ourselves, at least we'd know for sure something happened. So instead, all we got is Cohen is dead, nobody did an autopsy on the body, so it could've been poison. But all the people what die every day could've been poisoned, too, except those what get hit by a car or something. And Cohen was sick before, too.

"Mr. Guttman, I hope I'm not disturbing you."

"No, Mr. Carstairs, I'm just smoking a cigar."

"And avoiding the Golden Valley Irregulars?"

Guttman smiled sheepishly. "I don't know what to tell them," he explained.

"Is something up?"

"No, the opposite."

"If you'd like to talk, I'd be happy to listen," Mr. Carstairs said, sitting down in the easy chair across from Guttman.

"Well, it couldn't hurt. The problem is very simple. I think what I got to tell them is it don't look like nobody killed Cohen or Miss Walters."

"That's what I told you in the first place."

"I know," Guttman said. "And I never said something happened, actually. It was just that there was a possibility."

"Frankly, I never felt there was even that. It seemed so unlikely to me, from the very beginning. If you'll excuse me, I think it was a case of two rather bored and nosey women deciding to create a game, as it were, to amuse themselves. And they were successful in having you play their game for them."

"I suppose," Guttman said, examining the end of his cigar. "And I guess that's that." After a moment he asked Carstairs, "If you was so sure the whole thing was for nothing, how come you did all that work to help?"

"Am I still a suspect, Mr. Guttman?" Carstairs asked.

"I'm sorry." Guttman shook his head. "Maybe it's this cold I got. I'm not thinking straight. Even the cigar don't taste right." He didn't notice Carstairs wrinkle his nose.

"I'm not offended," Carstairs said. "But it's one of the reasons I agreed to help. I live here, Mr. Guttman. And I simply didn't want anyone going around whispering about this unfortunate situation, nor about me, for that matter."

"I could understand that."

"It's going to be difficult, explaining to them, isn't it?" Carstairs said sympathetically.

"Oy, I don't even like to think about it. I can see them. First Mrs. O'Rourke, she'll look at me and say, 'I don't understand.' And then Mrs. Kaplan. Who knows what she'll say? And I don't know what Miss Brady is gonna think. Mishkin, at least, won't make a fuss."

"Well, it may not be all that bad," Carstairs said comfortingly. "It's almost lunchtime. Are you going to tell them now?"

"Maybe in the morning, tomorrow," Guttman said. "Maybe I'll think about how I could say it by then. Besides, there's still something about it what bothers me. If I can figure that out, then maybe I'll know how to tell them."

"I won't say anything, then," Carstairs promised.

"I appreciate that."

"Not at all," Carstairs said, rising.

.   .   .

Lunch was awful. Mishkin, O'Rourke and Kaplan—the three of them at a table, saving a place for him. Guttman would have felt a little better if Miss Brady had been there, too. But there was no way to avoid them, so he carried his tray over and joined them.

"So how are you?" Mishkin asked.

"How should I be?"

"You went to the doctor, no? So what did he say?"

"He said I got a cold."

"He's a fine doctor, Dr. Morton," Agnes O'Rourke said.

"He might be a fine doctor, but I don't like him," Mishkin said.

"The pills he gave me help a little," Guttman said.

"Why don't you like him?" Mrs. O'Rourke asked.

"Because he's always talking about old people, like being old is a disease you should be ashamed of," Mishkin said.

"If you don't feel well, perhaps you should go home and go to bed," Mrs. Kaplan suggested to Guttman.

"I'm not sick enough to go to bed. It's just a cold." Perhaps in deference to his condition, they didn't pester him with questions about the investigation, and Guttman was very happy about that. If he could just get through the rest of the day. Maybe I should've stayed in the arts-and-crafts class, he thought. That way I'd have someplace to go and get away if I need to.

After lunch Guttman went outside to sit in the sun. The sun has vitamins, Mrs. O'Rourke explained. Actors sometimes took the same vitamins in pills, to make them look younger, she thought. Guttman watched the croquet game for a while, deciding that perhaps it might turn out to be interesting, after all. But not as much fun, probably, as bocce. Later, feeling restless, he got up and began wandering around the grounds. He wasn't really surprised to find himself, eventually, in front of Miss Brady's cottage, but once there, he hesitated before going up on the porch and knocking on the door.

"Mr. Guttman. Well, come on in. What did the doctor say?" Miss Brady asked, stepping back from the door.

"He said I got a cold. No temperature, though."

"Did he give you anything for it?" Guttman handed her the small plastic vial of pills. She removed one, looked at it and nodded. "These won't hurt," she said. "Would you like a cup of tea?"

"That would be very nice." He stood at the window, looking out through the trees toward the sky, while she put the water on to boil. "It's a nice place here. A good place for thinking."

"Too good, sometimes," Margaret Brady said.

"I wonder, do you have a pencil and a paper I could borrow?"

"Sure." She took a wire-bound notebook from the desk and gave it to him with a pencil.

Guttman sat down on the couch and put on his reading glasses. "I hope I won't be a bother, but I just wanted to do some thinking, and I didn't even realize I was walking this way," he said.

"Make yourself at home. I've got some reading I want to do, anyway, so don't worry about carrying on a conversation."

"Thank you," he said, wondering for just a moment why he should feel so relaxed with someone he'd known such a short time.

He thought for a moment, then wrote "The Nephew" at the top of the page. Okay, he thought, so now we got to consider. One thing is, Could he be the one what gave something to Cohen? For that we got a yes. He saw the uncle that day. So the next thing is, Does he got a reason? Well, he was worried about the money, but Cohen died after all that was settled already. So if he had a reason, it was over before Cohen died. So I'll put a question, and we'll see.

Okay, so now you got a partner. Again you could put a yes for having a chance to give Cohen something, because Cohen went to the Fancy Fair that day. And a reason? Well, you got maybe a better possibility for that. The insurance money for the business. Strauss didn't have enough money of his own to buy up the shares from Cohen, so if the business needed some money quick, maybe he thought to kill Cohen for the insurance. But that's a big maybe, Guttman realized. Carstairs said the business wasn't in really bad shape, so if that was so, probably

138

he could've gone to a bank for a loan. Okay, so put a maybe down for reasons.

"Mr. Guttman," Margaret Brady interrupted.

"Huh?"

"It slipped my mind. I was going to tell you about it this afternoon. During lunch I checked some of the files again. That business about Cohen's life insurance, remember?" Guttman nodded. "Well, I didn't find anything about it. No policy, nothing signing it over to the Center. Not a word about it."

"Is that normal?" Guttman asked.

"I really don't know. Maybe they sent the policy in to get it redeemed. I don't know."

"I see," Guttman said.

"Does it help?"

"I honestly don't know," Guttman told her. He looked back at his list. If the insurance wasn't settled yet for Miss Walters, then he could put a maybe down for the nephew. He could have had a reason, after all.

Carstairs. He lived at the Center, so he could've seen Cohen any time at all. For the first half of his question he had to put down a check mark. Carstairs had an opportunity. For the reason, the motive, however, that was something different. Carstairs is an intelligent man, Guttman thought. He also knew Miss Walters a long time. So would you figure he'd go and kill Cohen without figuring out how Miss Walters would feel about it? Also, he knew Cohen, and maybe they didn't agree about Cohen marrying Miss Walters, but when the subject came up, Carstairs didn't act like he hated Cohen or anything. Still, when people are in love . . . Guttman wrote down "Possible" next to Carstairs' name. He stared at the paper and sighed.

"Something wrong?" Miss Brady asked.

"It's this whole thing."

"Are you going to tell me, or do you want me to guess?" she asked, smiling.

"It wouldn't be hard to guess," Guttman told her. "But the thing is, none of it makes sense."

"How do you mean?"

"Well, the more I think about it, the less reason there is for anybody to kill Cohen when he died. Before, maybe. Could even be later on, too. But not when it happened."

"People don't always have what we'd consider good reasons when they kill someone," Miss Brady said.

"Maybe that's true. But if you don't know something happened in the first place, and you're only guessing, then it would be nice to be able to say, 'Look, here's a good reason, a good motive.' " Guttman got up from the couch and looked out the window. "And we don't got no good reasons."

"So it's all over?"

"I'm afraid so."

"You're sure?"

"As sure as I could be. Remember," he said with a smile he didn't really feel, "Sherlock Holmes I'm not. Anyway, I'll think on it some more." He looked at his watch and realized that it was almost time for him to meet Lois.

"I want to thank you for letting me sit here and do my thinking," he said.

"My pleasure. It's nice to have someone around. Come back any time," Margaret Brady said. "Even if you don't have any special thinking to do."

"Thank you." When he left, Guttman felt very tired, and he wondered how much of it was due to his cold. A little bit of thinking with your head don't make you so tired and depressed, he told himself. It must be the cold.

Lois' car was parked outside when he got there, but Guttman couldn't find his daughter. He wondered whether to just wait, or if she had gone inside looking for him. It's a little early, he thought, so maybe when she got here she figured she'd look for me. When he didn't find her in the main lounge, Guttman checked the snack lounge. Mishkin was at the usual table, finishing his last game of solitaire before going up to his room to prepare for dinner. He waved, and Guttman waved back. Well, he decided, so I'll wait at the car. She's bound to come back there sooner or later.

One look at his daughter's face as she came toward him and Guttman knew he was in trouble. And he had a pretty good idea, all of a sudden, what it was about. Lois got into the car, waited for him to close the door on the other side, and drove off. They were halfway home before she spoke to him.

"I don't know whether to be mad at you or . . . or what," she said. "How could you, Pop?"

"Aren't you at least gonna ask about my cold?" Guttman asked.

"I can hear your cold," Lois said. "Pop, how could you do something like this?"

Guttman didn't answer. In some ways, he thought, she's like her mother, and sometimes not saying anything is the best answer.

"I couldn't believe Dr. Morton at first. I thought it was some

141

kind of a joke. It was all a joke last week when you told me about this bright idea of yours—"

"It was Mrs. Kaplan's bright idea," Guttman corrected.

"And here I find you out running around playing detective," Lois went on. "Traipsing all over town bothering people because some crazy old woman was ranting and raving—"

"She was sick maybe, but she wasn't crazy," Guttman said sternly. Then he sneezed.

"Is the cold any worse?" Lois asked.

"About the same. The doctor gave me some pills."

"Did you take them?"

"Of course I took them," Guttman said. "That's why I went to the doctor in the first place, isn't it?"

"Better give them to me," Lois said. "I'll make sure you don't forget to take them when you're supposed to."

"I won't forget."

"Do you have a temperature? Let me feel," she said, reaching out with her right hand to touch his forehead.

"I don't have a temperature."

"After dinner you go right to bed."

"After dinner we'll see how I feel," Guttman told her.

"You're exasperating," Lois said. "Pop, what were you thinking about, playing detective like this? Didn't you realize that people might not like you poking around into their personal affairs?"

"I didn't want to poke into personal affairs, but . . ." he tried to explain.

"And what if, God forbid, there'd really been something to all of this?" Lois demanded. "What if it was something serious? Pop, don't you remember what happened in New York? Didn't you realize that you'd be in danger if this thing was real?"

"I wasn't in any danger," Guttman said, trying not to smile. What if it was for real, she had asked, not stopping to think that was why he was involved in the first place. But Lois wasn't listening to him, and in turn, he tried not to listen too carefully to her. Eventually, she'd talk herself out. And it was as good as over, anyway, so it really didn't matter.

· · ·

"I just can't trust you at all," Lois said to him as soon as he came down to breakfast the next morning. He was a little later than usual.

"Now what did I do?" Guttman asked.

"Your cold. Last night I told you to go to bed after dinner and you insisted on staying up. And now it's worse, right? I can tell by looking at you."

You could tell, Guttman thought, because I'm late this morning, that's all. "It's about the same," he lied. "It'll go away in a couple of days."

"It would get a lot better if you did what you were supposed to, instead of running all over town on a wild goose chase. Well," Lois said firmly, "this settles it."

"Settles what?"

"I'm telling Michael we can't make the trip this weekend. Now don't start," she said quickly. "Don't start telling me about being a burden. Being sick is different. I wouldn't go away if one of the children was sick, and I'm not going while you've got a bad cold like that."

"I'm not one of the children," Guttman reminded her.

"No, but you act like it sometimes. My father the detective," she said. And then Lois smiled, suddenly. "Honestly, you're impossible."

Guttman didn't argue with her. He really wasn't in a good position for it.

"Do you think you should be going in to the Center today?" Lois asked as she poured his coffee.

"I don't have a fever," he told her. "And I thought it would make sense, so the doctor could look at me and see if I should have more medicine or an injection."

"Well . . ."

"Honest, there's no fever. You could feel my forehead if you want," Guttman offered.

Lois did. "Well . . . okay. But call me—no, have the doctor call me after he looks at you. Then if he thinks you should be home in bed, I'll come and get you."

"Okay," Guttman said. Some battles you lost, he thought. "I been thinking," he said slowly.

"Oh? About what?"

"Well, I was thinking about the weekend . . ."

"It's all decided, Pop."

"I'm not arguing, really. But could I make a suggestion?"

"Okay," Lois said. "Make a suggestion."

"They got doctors at the Center, right?"

"Of course."

"Okay, so maybe it would be possible I could stay there over the weekend, if the cold isn't better."

"What do you mean?"

"Well, if they let me, then if I don't feel so good I could stay in bed and the doctors would take care of me."

"I don't know, Pop. I don't like to leave you when you're sick . . ."

"I'm not sick. I only got a cold, that's all. Not even the flu, the doctor said yesterday."

"Can you do that?" Lois asked after a moment.

"I don't know. I'll ask Dr. Morton. And if I could, it probably wouldn't be any money because of the Medicaire."

It wasn't until they were in the car that Lois relented. "If the doctor says it's all right, then I'll go along with it," she said. "But you ask him to call me right after he examines you, all right?"

"I'll talk to him first thing," Guttman told her.

He watched her turn the corner and pull away. It's nice, in a way, he thought, having somebody worrying about you. But it's also a nuisance. He started across the wide two-way street when the light changed. Later he thought that it was living in New York that did it. In New York, no matter what the street, if you were smart, you always looked both ways.

He saw the car when it was still some distance away, before it entered the intersection. It was going too fast, and it was going against the traffic light. Then, even as someone yelled for him to look out, Guttman knew that the car wasn't staying in the right lane, that it was swerving toward him. He ran, frustrated that he couldn't move more quickly, that he hardly seemed to be moving at all, and then he stumbled and fell at the curb, landing heavily on his hip as he reached the sidewalk.

His view obscured by a mailbox, Guttman saw the car's

front wheel miss his leg by a foot as it swerved and the tire bounced against the curb; he saw the seemingly massive body of the car speed by so close that he could have almost reached out and touched it, lying there as he was. The tires screeched, and the car sped away down the broad street.

For a moment he couldn't breathe, his heart pounding, his head throbbing. And then there was the reaction, the sudden weakness, the feeling that his face was flushed when somehow he knew that he had gone pale . . .

"Mister, are you all right? Jesus, I thought that nut was going to kill you . . ."

"He must have been drunk," a woman said indignantly.

Guttman looked up.

"Are you all right?" The first voice belonged to a young man, bearded and long-haired, wearing jeans and a sweatshirt. That was the voice that had first yelled for him to look out.

"Should we call the police?" the woman asked. "A mad-man," she said.

"I'm okay," Guttman said, surprised at how normal his voice sounded to him. "He just scared me, that's all."

"Better lie still," the young man said. "You took a pretty hard fall."

"I'm okay," Guttman repeated. "Maybe a couple of black and blue marks is all." His right wrist seemed sore, and his knee, as if he had scraped it. And there was a duller pain in his thigh. He sat up.

"Are you sure you should be getting up?" the woman asked. She was in her fifties, a black woman. "Kids," she said. "None of them have any respect," ignoring the young man who was standing over Guttman.

"I'm okay. Maybe you could help me getting up . . ." The young man took his arm. On his feet, Guttman swayed for just an instant, then felt better. He exhaled slowly, breathed deeply. "I'm fine," he said with relief.

"You should see a doctor," the woman said.

"It's funny," Guttman told them. "I was just going inside there, to see a doctor about a cold I got."

"It's a good thing you're able to move so fast," the young man said, still holding on to Guttman's arm.

"I felt like I wasn't moving at all."

"You moved, man. Believe me. When I first yelled, I didn't think you had a chance. Did you get the guy's number?"

"No." Guttman shook his head.

"Neither did I." He looked at the woman, and she shook her head. "Listen, are you sure you're all right?" he asked.

"I'm fine," Guttman told him. "And I'm gonna see a doctor now, anyway, so he could double-check." The young man released his arm. "I want to thank you," Guttman said.

"Forget it. I'm just sorry I didn't get his license number."

"Well, I'm glad you yelled, anyway. For that, I certainly thank you."

"I think we should call the police," the woman said.

"Maybe from inside," Guttman said. "Thanks again." He took a few tentative steps, then walked fairly briskly away to the front doors of the Golden Valley Senior Citizens' Center.

He went straight to the library, wanting a few minutes to gain more complete control over himself and not wanting to see anyone until then. He sat down and carefully pulled up his trouser leg to look at his knee. Scraped a little, but not too bad. He tested his wrist, and found the stiffness that he'd felt earlier disappearing already. I'm lucky I didn't break a couple of bones, he thought. Casey Stengel, from the Mets, fell down walking on a ramp once, and he broke a hip and had to walk with a cane for a long time. All I got is a bruise, probably. After a few moments he decided to light a cigar.

Somebody tried to kill me, he thought calmly. I knew it the minute I saw the car. Somebody tried to kill me. So how come, all of a sudden, I feel so good? Because you was right. Because there is something. Somebody killed Mr. Cohen, and Miss Walters maybe. Two people is dead, and knowing it makes you feel good? Nu, Guttman, a bloodthirsty person you're getting to be. Okay, so not bloodthirsty. But now, at least, they're gonna know you were right. Lois even, thinking you're dumb for doing this, and Dr. Morton with his giving orders to stop.

146

Okay, he told himself, so now think. You know somebody's trying to kill you, but you don't know who it is. And that, he thought with a smile, could be a nice thing to find out. Well, he had some time to think about it. If he didn't go out again, he wouldn't get hit by a car. And as for lunch, he'd go to the cafeteria line like he always did, and nobody could poison him because they wouldn't know what he was going to eat, and they couldn't put anything in all the food.

This time Dr. Morton saw him immediately. "Mr. Guttman, how's your cold this morning?"

"I don't think it's much better," Guttman told him. "Maybe even a little worse."

"Any fever?"

"I don't think so," Guttman said, opening his mouth to accept the thermometer.

"Breathe," Dr. Morton said, holding the end of the stethoscope against Guttman's chest. "Again. Have to look out for congestion. It doesn't take much for a simple cold to develop into pneumonia. That's one of our biggest problems with older people, you know. Ah, no fever."

"That's good," Guttman said.

"You still have some of the medication I prescribed for you yesterday," Dr. Morton said, looking at a file card. "Just keep on taking them, and we'll have another look at you tomorrow."

"Thank you," Guttman said. "I got two things to ask, please."

"Yes?"

"The first is a personal thing. My daughter, Lois . . ."

"I'm sorry I had to speak to her yesterday, Mr. Guttman. I'm sure you understand, something like this, well . . ."

"I understand."

"You see," the doctor continued, "I have the feeling that you're a strong-minded man, Mr. Guttman. And, well, I just wasn't sure, after our talk yesterday, that you were really going to give up this little . . . investigation of yours."

"Naturally, you got to do what you think is best," Guttman said. "That wasn't the thing, though. You see, my daughter and her husband, they was planning on going away for the weekend. They got the kids staying with other people, but now, with this cold, she wouldn't leave me by myself."

"Well, I don't think your cold's really serious . . ."

"That's what I told her. Only she's worried, and she don't listen to me. So what I was wondering, is it possible for a person to stay here at the Center for a weekend maybe? I mean, this is like a hospital, no? I could stay until they come back on Sunday. That way she wouldn't worry about me being sick, because of you and the other doctors . . ."

"Well . . ." Dr. Morton thought for a moment, reaching for his pipe. "It's been done before, although we try not to make a habit of it. Still, you're cooperating with me, so I suppose it's the least I can do. Of course, you won't be in the hospital wing. I don't think that's necessary. But if you should take a turn for the worse, the staff will be here, as you say."

"I appreciate it very much," Guttman said.

"I'll make the arrangements."

"Thank you," Guttman said, rising.

"You mentioned two things, I think . . ."

"Oy, I almost forgot. The other thing is, would you do me a favor and call my daughter?"

"Call her?"

"She was saying this morning I should stay home in bed, and I promised you'd call her after you examined me so she'd know I was okay."

"Of course," Dr. Morton said, smiling. "You know, sometimes the children are far more trouble than our residents."

"Children is like that," Guttman answered, smiling back at the doctor. "And I appreciate very much how you're helping me."

"Not at all," Dr. Morton said, picking up his phone to tell the nurse out front to call Mr. Guttman's daughter, please.

Guttman was a little surprised to see all of his Irregulars assembled and waiting for him. Of course, he realized, they don't know what's happened. And Miss Brady and Mr. Carstairs is the only ones knowing that I was thinking about quitting

148

yesterday. So they're here to find out for sure. And the others is just here regular.

"The ten o'clock scholar," Mrs. Kaplan said.

"I had to see the doctor," Guttman explained. "About my cold."

"How is it?" Mishkin asked.

"Maybe a little worse." Guttman sipped his tea. "I see everybody's here."

"We thought it would be nice to find out what was happening," Mrs. Kaplan said.

"Have you worked things out, Mr. Guttman?" Agnes O'Rourke asked.

"Not exactly."

"That's a big help," Mrs. Kaplan said.

"The clues are there," Guttman admitted. "Only I can't put them together right."

"The clues? But yesterday . . ." Mr. Carstairs was surprised.

"Yesterday was yesterday," Guttman told him. He looked at Miss Brady, who was smiling. So how come she isn't surprised? he wondered.

"So what do we do now?" Mishkin asked.

"Now we got to get some time," Guttman said slowly, trying to formulate his ideas.

"Time for what?" Mrs. O'Rourke asked.

"Time to get the evidence. To get proof."

"You mean you know who did it?" Mrs. Kaplan demanded.

"I got a pretty good idea," Guttman lied. They stared at him for a moment, and he took another swallow of his tea.

Mrs. Kaplan regained her voice first. "Who?" she asked.

"That's where the proof comes in," he told her.

"What kind of proof?"

"You can't just say a person killed someone and then not be able to prove it," Guttman lectured. "We got to get proof to go to the police with, and that's the hard part."

"How are we going to manage that?" Miss Brady asked.

"I think we got it already. But putting it together is the hard part."

149

"You're being rather cryptic, Mr. Guttman," Carstairs said.

"I'm telling you what I can."

"You said there'd be no secrets," Mrs. Kaplan reminded him.

"I'm not keeping secrets. Everybody knows the same things I know." It wasn't true, but still, he didn't know who had killed Cohen. Or why.

"I'm afraid I don't understand," Agnes O'Rourke said. "What are we going to do now?"

"I'm gonna sit and figure things out, if I can," Guttman told her.

"And what are the rest of us supposed to do while you sit and think?" Dora Kaplan demanded. "You think this is like a Nero Wolfe book, where the genius solves the mystery while everyone else is in the dark?"

"I don't know this Nero Wolfe," Guttman said.

They continued to look at him, waiting for him to explain, while Guttman found himself wondering whether this Wolfe was a Jewish detective. He'd known some Jews named Wolfe, and it might be interesting to read about one who was a detective. Except he'd never known anyone named Nero.

"Is there anything we can do to help?" Margaret Brady asked finally.

"I been thinking about that. I think what we got to do is make sure we could get some time. Also, maybe we could get the killer to put down his guard."

"But how are we going to do that when we don't know who the killer is?" Mrs. O'Rourke asked reasonably.

"We work with everybody," Guttman explained.

"But how?"

"By talking to everybody that's involved. We got to let the killer think we don't know who it is . . ."

"That shouldn't be hard," Mrs. Kaplan said.

"So here's what I got in mind. For Mr. Carstairs, if you could go back to the Fancy Fair today and maybe talk to Strauss, or else tomorrow, and tell him how you're sorry you brung me along the first time, and that you're sure I don't think he's the killer, or anything . . ."

"I suppose I could do that," Carstairs said after a moment.

"Good," Guttman went on quickly. "And Mrs. Kaplan, maybe you could call to the nephew's wife and also make an apology for bringing me there, and tell her the same kind of thing Mr. Carstairs is gonna tell Strauss."

"I should say, Mr. Guttman, that when I see Eli Strauss, I'll be quite sincere if I tell him that I don't think you know what you're doing," Carstairs said.

"You're entitled to your opinion," Guttman conceded.

"That is my opinion."

"If you think that way, why have you been working with us on this, assuming you have?" Mrs. O'Rourke demanded.

"Because I agreed to help, and I won't go back on my word. But I'll be very glad when this is all over."

"I'm sure you will," Mrs. Kaplan suggested.

"Is there anything else here that involves me?" Carstairs asked.

"That's all," Guttman said. "But I appreciate how you're being honest with me, Mr. Carstairs. I want you should know I don't take it personal that you think I'm wrong."

"Good," Carstairs said, "because I did not intend it in a personal way."

"It sounded personal to me," Mrs. Kaplan said as Carstairs left them.

"I still don't trust him," Mrs. O'Rourke reminded them.

"He was in love with Miss Walters," Miss Brady said evenly. "I think all of this upsets him because of that."

"Still . . ."

"Enough," Guttman said sternly.

"I agree," Mishkin said. "You got something for the rest of us to do?"

"It would help if you talk to the people here at the Center again. I'll help with that, since I'll be here over the weekend even," Guttman added, explaining about Lois' worrying and his cold.

"Okay," Mishkin said. "But what are we supposed to talk to people about?"

"Talk to them about how you're looking for proof now, only

you don't know who I figure done it. That's the truth, so it should be an easy thing. The only thing, maybe we should wait until tomorrow. My daughter's going to San Francisco then, and if Dr. Morton hears we're still investigating, he wouldn't be able to call her again and get me in trouble."

"Anything special for me?" Margaret Brady asked.

"Only if you could go look at all the records again. Maybe there's something we didn't think about the first time."

"On the premise that if you look long enough, maybe you'll find something?" Miss Brady asked with a small smile.

"I don't know about a premise. I'm just hoping a little."

Guttman spent the rest of the morning quietly reading the newspapers and watching still another game of croquet on the lawn, and trying to figure out what it was that he could have learned which made a killer want to see him dead too.

After lunch he went outside again, and tried to decide whether a visit to Miss Brady and perhaps a game or two of chess would help, or whether he should sit with Mishkin and play pinochle.

"Deciding where to put the bocce courts?"

"Oh, Mr. Bowsenior, I didn't hear you."

"Crepe-soled shoes. I wear them all the time," Mr. Bowsenior said, standing next to him and looking out across the back lawn. "Under the trees, back there," he said. "Not such a good idea to have the court right out in the sun. It's a slow game. Doesn't do, at our age, to spend too much time in the direct rays of the sun. Especially in summer." He patted his pockets, looking for a cigar. "Must have left them with Ursula. Come on over for a while."

"Thank you," Guttman said. "But I got a cigar."

"Join us anyway," Mr. Bowsenior said, misunderstanding.

"I was going to," Guttman said, falling into step with him.

Mrs. Bowsenior was sitting in a lawn chair under the trees. In front of her was a small easel. She smiled up at Guttman as he stepped around to look at the painting. Guttman expected to see what she was looking at—the trees, the main house behind them. Instead, he saw mountains and a desert.

"After two years here," Mrs. Bowsenior explained, "I've painted just about every view of the place I like. So mostly now I work from photographs of places we've been to."

"It's very pretty," Guttman said.

"Thank you."

"I guess you seen a lot of places," he said.

"Oh, just about every place, I guess," Mr. Bowsenior said.

"He's exaggerating, but just a little. Actually, we've moved around quite a bit. New York, Philadelphia, New Orleans, Chicago, San Francisco, here, two glorious years in Hawaii . . ."

"And assorted other locales," Mr. Bowsenior added.

"I'm sure it was very interesting," Guttman said. Aside from his boyhood before coming to America, he'd lived in New York. And now here.

"It has its advantages, too. Around here, for example, just about everyone will come over once in a while to talk about their hometowns. Maggie Brady will come by when she feels nostalgic for Boston, although she hasn't been there in twenty years probably, and neither have we," Mr. Bowsenior said.

"And Mr. Clancy, who for some reason I'll never understand likes to remember living in Detroit. Ugh, what a city," Mrs. Bowsenior said.

"And then, Sam Cohen used to like to talk about New Orleans once in a while," her husband continued.

"He loved that city, but he was there long before we were," Mrs. Bowsenior told Guttman. "So we really didn't remember it the same way."

"Remember when Dr. Morton arrived? Cohen greeted him like a long-lost brother."

"You're exaggerating again."

"I always exaggerate," Mr. Bowsenior told Guttman. "And she loves to tell me so."

"Did Cohen know Dr. Morton from before he came here?" Guttman asked.

"I think so . . ." Mr. Bowsenior said.

154

"Didn't he say something about . . . ?" Mrs. Bowsenior added.

"It was years ago, he said . . ."

"Can't remember it exactly . . ."

"Right. But he sure liked to talk about New Orleans, although I don't think he'd been there in I don't know how many years. But it's a nice city."

"Too hot in the summer, though," Mrs. Bowsenior said as if that explained everything.

"Good restaurants."

"You know, I'm pretty sure . . . No, I remember."

"What, dear?"

"I forget. Damn," Mrs. Bowsenior said. "Well, let's see what we can get on the radio."

For half an hour Guttman smoked his cigar and listened to some kind of violin music. It isn't so bad, he thought. Long hair could be okay if you just listen while you're relaxing, or painting like Mrs. Bowsenior. He wondered whether she was in the class with Mrs. Kaplan. Finally, though, he decided to go inside and play some pinochle with Mishkin. This kind of music, he thought, could either put you to sleep or make you restless. And he began to feel restless.

That evening, from the moment Lois picked him up, he had to make a special effort to minimize the effects of his cold. So while he felt sleepy, and his hip was beginning to stiffen up quite a bit, Guttman forced himself to sit in the living room and watch television with the family. His ruse must have worked, because Lois said nothing about staying home for the weekend. Indeed, she spent much of the evening packing for the trip. By the time he went to his room for the night, Guttman was very tired, but he wasn't sure if it was all because of the cold, or from trying so hard not to look sick. Before he went to bed he packed the few things he'd need for the weekend, including the Sherlock Holmes book and a portable radio borrowed from Joseph. He put the bag on a chair, then looked in his closet to find what he needed.

The cane was surprisingly heavy. Like a fungo bat used in

baseball, a policeman had once explained, it was hollowed out in part and refilled with lead. Guttman had asked for it as a souvenir. He'd never expected to really need it. Now, with his hip becoming more stiff, it would be useful. Thinking about the events of the day, Guttman found it hard to fall asleep.

Lois asked about the cane as soon as she saw it in the morning. He'd known that she would, of course. Guttman had thought about trying to hide it, but she'd have seen it when she drove him to the Center, and besides, the leg was even more stiff now than when he'd gone to bed. He found it really helped quite a bit.

"I didn't want to tell you," he explained. "I knew you'd worry."

"What happened?" Lois asked.

"A stupid thing. I'm walking along in the street, and I don't look where I'm going. I tripped over the curb."

"Are you all right? I mean—"

"Lois, it was yesterday, not this morning getting out of bed. I got a bruise, that's all. The doctor looked at it," he added, hoping that she wouldn't suddenly decide to call Dr. Morton. "If it worries you I'm using the cane, I'll leave it here," he said. "I don't need it that bad."

"No, Pop, as long as you're all right."

"You know, Michael," Guttman said to his son-in-law, "it's a good thing you're taking her away. I heard about parents what protect the children too much, how they worry all the time until the child gets a neurotic something, but never did I hear about it like this, where it's the child worrying about the parent."

"I'm inclined to think you're right," Michael said.

"All right, the two of you. That's enough," Lois said, a bit embarrassed.

Lois had a few more words of caution for him before she drove out of the Golden Valley driveway. She'd insisted on dropping him at the door, because it might be hard for him to handle both the overnight bag and the cane. Remembering yesterday, Guttman didn't argue.

"Pop, I'll call over the weekend, and—"

"If you call me, I wouldn't answer," Guttman told her.

"But, Pop—"

"No discussion. You gave me a number to call if anything happens, which it won't. Where the children are, they got a number for you, too. So just forget about worrying and enjoy the weekend, that's all. Besides," he teased, "you're a big girl. You could go a whole weekend without talking to your Poppa."

"Okay," she said. "You win." She kissed him on the cheek, and Guttman stood at the front door of the Center and watched her drive off.

Inside, he went straight to Dr. Morton's office, where he was expected. The nurse told him to leave his bag with her and to go right in. Dr. Morton looked at the cane but didn't ask about it. Lots of the people at the Center, Guttman knew, used canes. The doctor apologized for having to hurry, then took Guttman's temperature, listened again to his chest, and wrote out a new prescription.

"Well, it still doesn't look bad," the doctor said. "But I'm glad you're going to be here over the weekend. You can never be too sure. This is a new prescription, a bit stronger than what you were taking, but there's no need to worry."

Guttman thanked him, feeling a bit concerned about his health for the first time since he'd caught cold, and went outside. The nurse offered to carry the bag while she showed him to his room, but Guttman carried it himself as he followed her up the one flight of stairs. The room wasn't very big, but it was nice enough, and he was only going to be there for two nights. The bed was a hospital-type, higher than usual, with a motor to raise it and lower it so that you could sit up more easily. There was a dresser with a mirror over it, a comfortable-looking vinyl-covered chair, and a small table with a lamp on it next to the bed.

After the nurse left him, Guttman unpacked, putting everything he had brought into one drawer of the dresser and hanging up his sport jacket in the closet. Then he left the toilet kit he had borrowed from Michael, an old one of his, and put it in the bathroom. He took the cane with him when he went downstairs.

In the snack lounge he found Mrs. Kaplan sitting alone at their usual table. She pretended not to notice him until he actually sat down, and then all she said was good morning. Guttman sipped his tea and wondered what was wrong. Finally he asked, "So where is everybody today?"

"Doing what you asked them to do, I suppose," Mrs. Kaplan said.

"I got to go to the pharmacy to get some more medicine," he said.

"Is your cold still bothering you?"

"A little. Like I said, I'm gonna stay here for the weekend."

"You could have come and stayed with us," she suggested. "There's plenty of room."

"I could also have stayed home, only my Lois was worried I'm sick. So here, she figured, there's doctors all over, so she said she'd go on the trip."

"I suppose that makes sense," Mrs. Kaplan acknowledged. "By the way, I spoke to Mrs. Cole last night."

"You did?"

"Yes."

"And?"

"And what?"

"And what happened?"

"I told her what you told me to say," Mrs. Kaplan explained.

"And what did she say?"

"Well, of course she wanted to know what you thought had happened, who might have done something to Mr. Cohen, but naturally," Mrs. Kaplan added, "since I didn't have any idea whatsoever of what you were thinking, I couldn't tell her."

"That's good," Guttman said.

"Now that I've done my job, maybe you could tell me what this is all about?"

"I got to go to the pharmacy and get the new medicine," Guttman said. He left as quickly as he could, surprised that Mrs. Kaplan hadn't mentioned the cane.

Half an hour later he was back. The others drifted in, but no one seemed anxious to talk to him, although Mishkin, when he arrived, suggested that they play cards. For variety, they found a regular deck and played gin rummy. The day dragged. After lunch he walked over to visit Miss Brady. She was sitting on the porch of her cabin, reading. He stood there for a moment watching her, and then coughed involuntarily.

"Mr. Guttman. I was kind of hoping you'd drop by."

"I thought I'd see if you learned anything new."

"I was going to come over to the main house in a while. But I'm afraid there's nothing new."

"Well, I didn't really expect it. You know what I keep wondering, though . . ."

"Nope."

"Well," Guttman said, climbing the steps to the porch, "I keep wondering why it is that somebody killed Cohen when they did."

"Would you like something, maybe a cup of tea?"

"Thank you, no. I had already. But you have, if you want."

"Maybe later," she said. "Go ahead with what you were saying."

"Well, it's just that it don't make sense to kill Cohen when he died."

"The other day you said that was why you didn't think anyone killed Cohen at all," Miss Brady reminded him.

"That was then. But now I figure there's something we didn't find out about, or else we did and I'm not sure what it is."

"I can't think of anything," Miss Brady said after a moment. Guttman shrugged. "What's with the cane?"

"Oh, I fell down yesterday, and my leg is a little sore. Did you happen to see Mr. Carstairs today?"

"I saw him leaving this morning, when I went over to see if there was any mail."

"Well, maybe he went to Fancy Fair to see Strauss, or maybe the nephew."

"Could be. I didn't talk to him."

"Well, I'll go back to the main building," Guttman said. "Maybe I'll see him there." When he'd first come over, he had thought about playing chess. Now he didn't think he'd enjoy it. The cold was, indeed, getting worse, and he was having a little trouble breathing.

"I understand you'll be with us for the weekend," Miss Brady said.

"Yes. My daughter's away, and she didn't want me staying alone, because of the cold."

"I guess I'll see you at dinner, then."

"That would be very nice," Guttman said. "I'll look for you."

Guttman spent the next two hours in the library, alternately picking up the newspaper to read and finding himself drifting off into thought. Things were working themselves out very slowly. One thing after another, the ideas began to fall into place. But there was still no proof. I could say I'm guessing, he thought, except that it's the only way it makes sense. And it's stretching things. Still, it could be.

About four o'clock he went back to the lounge to join Mishkin for a few hands of cards. Mrs. O'Rourke and Mrs. Kaplan were there, too. Guttman had the feeling they stopped talking when they saw him, and it bothered him. It could also be, he thought, my imagination. A little before the day members were scheduled to leave, Mr. Carstairs joined them.

"I saw Strauss," he said, not bothering to sit down with them at the table.

"So what did he say?"

"Hardly anything. I don't think he's concerned at all."

"What do you mean concerned?" Mishkin asked.

"Just that I think he doesn't feel anything happened to Samuel Cohen, and he's not worried whether we investigate the matter or not. I just don't think he cares."

"Well, at least you talked to him," Guttman said.

"Yes. I don't think he believes it, though."

"He doesn't believe I got an idea who done it?"

"He doesn't believe anyone did anything," Carstairs replied. "He and I agree about that."

"You already gave us your opinion," Mrs. O'Rourke said.

"It's all right," Guttman said. "I got the feeling everything is set now."

"Then you're going to tell us?" Mrs. O'Rourke asked expectantly.

"Not until Monday," Guttman said.

"I should have known," Mrs. Kaplan sighed. "Guttman with his secrets."

"That's the way it's got to be," Guttman said.

After a while Mrs. O'Rourke walked outside with Mrs. Kaplan, to wait with her for her ride. The weekend had officially begun.

The lounge and recreation areas emptied quickly, as the residents returned to their rooms to prepare for dinner. They didn't have to go this quickly, Guttman knew, but he had been told that everyone did. It was, perhaps, just that they didn't like seeing the day members being picked up by their families and taken home. And this way they had time for a short nap, if they wished, before dinner and the evening activity that followed it. Tonight was movie night and a western was scheduled, which pleased most of the men and few of the women. The men, outnumbered, considered this something of a special event.

It took Guttman only ten minutes to wash and prepare himself for the evening. Then, with nothing else to do for nearly an hour, he turned on the radio and sat in the easy chair, listening to the news and weather reports. He wasn't paying as much attention to the news lately as he used to in New York. He remembered going into Bensky's candy store every morning and buying his newspapers, and then when the weather was nice, sitting in the park and reading the paper from front to back. He had always been interested in the stories about science, or doctors making new discoveries. And he went to the library fairly often, too. Here, he realized, the only book he had looked at was Sherlock Holmes. And some of the chess stuff, of course.

I got to get more interested in things again, Guttman told himself. The more interested a person is, the better off he is. Then he don't get bored. There's always something that's important, that makes him feel curious, almost like having a reason for doing things. So for Mrs. Kaplan and Mrs. O'Rourke with the oil painting only, and Mishkin with the playing cards, something like playing detective is a big deal. And for you, Guttman? Okay, for me too. He smiled when he realized that he'd been so busy thinking he hadn't heard the news broadcast.

He was too early getting down for dinner. The dining room was empty, although it was a quarter to six, just fifteen minutes before dinner was supposed to be served. He was a little surprised to find white cloths on the tables, and everything set up with plates and silverware. But only about half of the tables were prepared that way. I guess, he thought, not so many people live here full-time as I thought. I never even seen all these lights on in the building, he realized, because I never been here at night. It's almost like I was never here before at all.

"Nu, Guttman, you're so hungry you're here first thing?" Mishkin asked.

"There wasn't nothing to do in the room, so I came down. I notice you're here, too. What's the matter, you didn't eat enough for lunch?"

"What they feed me, it don't matter. Nothing has a taste any more." Mishkin shook his head and sat down on the couch with Guttman. He was wearing a light-gray suit and a white shirt, but no tie. I guess, Guttman thought, it's a good thing to change clothes a little bit for the evening. The English, he remembered, used to dress up in tuxedos for dinner even if they was in the jungle. It was civilization, they used to say.

"So we might as well go in," Mishkin said after a while.

"It's not too early? Miss Brady said maybe we'd all have dinner together," Guttman said, not sure that was what she meant.

"We don't have to eat right away. But I like to get the same waitress. Always polite, a very nice girl. Some of them, you don't like to ask for a cup of tea after you eat, the way they act."

"They got waitresses?"

"Only for dinner."

Mishkin led him to a table against the back wall, and

Guttman sat so he could see the entrance. It's all so different, he thought, even though the cafeteria area was still there, with the steam table. There was a menu now, though, a mimeographed sheet of paper held to a heavier piece of cardboard with a paper clip. Chicken, pot roast and fish.

Margaret Brady arrived just behind Mrs. O'Rourke. Guttman was surprised that both of them looked so different, until he remembered that he had dressed up a little too. He was wearing his sport jacket instead of just the sweater. Miss Brady was wearing a pale-blue dress that made her seem even taller and slimmer than usual, and while her hair, cropped short, was the same, somehow it looked softer. It must be the make-up, Guttman thought, realizing that she had lipstick on and some stuff around her eyes. Just a little, but it looked nice. Mrs. O'Rourke looked okay too, but maybe there was a little too much rouge on the cheeks, he thought.

Throughout dinner Mishkin and Mrs. O'Rourke seemed pleased that they had a guest, and told Guttman stories about the weekend routine, about the other residents, and discussed the movie for the evening. A movie, on a larger screen, was much better than watching television, even the color TV. It was more like going out. When they finished eating, Mishkin suggested that they hurry a bit, to be sure of getting good seats for the picture. It was important, he explained, to seat yourself where you could see the screen clearly but where you were neither too close nor too far from the speakers, which didn't function consistently.

"Are you watching the movie, too?" Guttman asked Miss Brady.

"Sure. I love westerns."

"So we'll all sit together," Guttman said, wondering why he felt as though he was blushing. The Bowseniors waved to him from their table as he followed the others out of the dining room. Was that a bottle of wine on their table? They're allowed to drink? So why not? They're grown-up people, ain't they?

"I could use a smoke," Miss Brady said as they returned to the main lounge. The furniture had been rearranged, the couches and chairs turned around so that they faced a large screen on a metal stand. The projector was at the back of the room.

"They rent the movies," Mrs. O'Rourke said. "Just like the movie stars when they have a private showing."

"I didn't know," Guttman said, taking a cigar from his pocket.

"You have to smoke outside," Miss Brady told him.

"But during the day . . ."

"During the day the air conditioning is turned up higher, so it doesn't matter. But it gets stuffy during a movie, so there's a rule about smoking when a movie's scheduled," she explained. "Come on, we'll go outside. They'll hold our seats for us."

Guttman followed her out to the portico. As he struck a match to light his cigar, he saw that Miss Brady was just holding her cigarette, and he realized, embarrassed, that she was waiting for him. He held the match out for her, noticing the way the flame lit up her whole face as she leaned down, and he smelled her perfume. It was dark outside, and very quiet. Standing there together, neither of them speaking, Guttman felt sad in a strange way. For the first time, really, he was personally upset that Samuel Cohen and Miss Walters were dead. And for the first time he truly understood how Miss Walters could have been so upset. He remembered, more strongly than he wanted to, how it had been when his Sarah had died.

Fifteen minutes after the movie was over, almost all of the residents had gone to their rooms. It wasn't ten o'clock yet, but it seemed that this, too, was normal. On movie nights, if anyone wanted to stay up later, watching television, they did it in their own rooms. It took too long to put the couches and chairs back into position, Mishkin explained. Guttman declined an offer to play a few hands of pinochle and said goodnight to the others.

He tried to read for a while, but it was difficult for him to concentrate. He listened to the last few innings of the Dodger game, then went to the bathroom to get ready for bed. It was very quiet there, and he felt very strange. Even worse than the first night at Lois', where at least he'd known there was family, known that the room would be his from now on. He put his socks and underwear in the plastic bag Lois had given him and then put that in the suitcase in the closet. Then, in his pajamas and robe, he sat in the easy chair, listening to the radio and he tried to read. At ten-thirty there was a knock on the door.

"Come in," he said.

"Mr. Guttman?" He didn't know the nurse, but of course he really hadn't seen many of them. As a rule, they stayed in the clinic area during the day, as if not to remind anyone where they really were.

"Yes," he said.

"Hi. I'm Nurse Thompson. Dr. Morton left a prescription for you." She was a pretty girl, not much past twenty, he thought. Her uniform was very clean, and starched.

"I would have come sooner, but one of the patients wasn't feeling well and I just finished taking care of her. I hope I'm not disturbing you."

"No, I was just reading. What's the medicine?"

"For your cold," she said, holding out a very small paper cup with two pills in it.

Guttman took the cup and put it on the night table.

"You'll have to take them now," the girl explained.

"Before I go to sleep," he said.

"I'm sorry, but it's regulations. All medication is to be taken immediately."

"Half an hour's gonna make a difference?"

"Regulations," the nurse said, showing a little annoyance.

Guttman looked at her for a moment, then shrugged and put the pills in his mouth. Reluctantly, he sipped water from the paper cup she held out to him.

"Thank you," she said, smiling a little. He could almost hear her thinking "Old people." "Good night," she said. Guttman just nodded at her. As soon as she was gone he went into the bathroom.

He tried reading again, but he still couldn't concentrate, and he found himself growing sleepy. Maybe it's all the medicine I took today, he thought. No, it's just a long day, and I didn't sleep so well last night, with the cold and all the thinking. He noticed that there was no lock on the door. I guess they're afraid somebody could lock himself in and then get sick and they couldn't come and help him. Even though this wasn't the hospital wing, there was a button next to the bed that said "Ring for nurse." He opened the door a crack and looked out. It was a very heavy door. From inside, you can't hear anything going on out there, so it must be practically soundproof both ways. Well, he thought, when you get old, sometimes you cough a lot, so this way nobody keeps anybody else up at night, I guess. He turned on the small lamp by the bed and then went back to the door to turn off the overhead light.

Now there's a problem. It probably wouldn't be tonight, but there's no sense taking chances. But no locks, and even if there was one, it would be a mistake to use it. Dental floss. He'd never used it until Lois had given him some one day. There was a package in the toilet kit. Guttman tied one end around the doorknob, looped it around the metal bedpost, and after cutting it from the plastic container, tied the other end around his wrist. Now if he fell asleep, he'd have something to warn him if the door opened.

He turned the portable radio up a bit, pulled the blanket over his feet to keep them warm, and sat back in the bed to wait. Then he remembered, and got the cane, laying it beside him on the bed. Now all he had to do was wait. And think. Do I want it now or later? he thought. Do I want to get it over, or to wait? Do I get a choice?

———————

Guttman woke up slowly. Not with a sudden jerk, as if he'd been startled. He blinked several times, then froze in sharp fear. The dental-floss string had worked.

"I'm sorry I woke you," he said, examining the string.

"I'm sorry I fell asleep," Guttman answered.

"You couldn't stay awake all night. It wouldn't be good for you. I just thought I'd drop in and see that you were all right."

"I'm fine."

"Did you take your medication?"

"I took it," Guttman said. "The nurse made a fuss and watched."

"Yes, they always do," he said. "This was very clever," he commented, holding up the string. "You surprise me, Mr. Guttman."

"I surprise you? What do you think you do to me?"

"I was sure you'd be fast asleep."

"I was."

"Yes, but I didn't think something like this"—he touched the string again—"would be enough to wake you."

"It was."

"That's what surprises me. You should have been in a very deep sleep. I'll have to check on the supplies. The medication may have lost its potency. Still, you look quite tired."

"I'm okay," Guttman told him.

"You're quite a character, aren't you?" Dr. Morton said, leaning back against the door, his arms crossed.

"I could say the same about you."

"Yes, I suppose so," the doctor answered, stroking his mustache. "Wouldn't you like to lie back and rest a bit?"

"What happens then?"

"Nothing, really."

"What do you mean, nothing, really?"

"Nothing for you to worry about. Once I know you're resting comfortably, I'll leave."

"You could go now," Guttman said, with a trace of a smile. He tightened his grip on the cane.

"I'll wait, thank you."

"What happens if I yell for help?"

"I doubt that anyone would hear you. The walls are quite well insulated. And all of the nearby rooms are empty."

"I could ring for the nurse," Guttman suggested.

"It's out of order, I'm afraid."

"So it's just the two of us."

"Yes. Just the two of us."

"What if I don't go to sleep. What if I stay up all night."

"There's always tomorrow night, Mr. Guttman. You can't stay awake forever. And you have been taking the medication all day, haven't you? Yes," the doctor said, glancing at the plastic vial that had held the pills. "You'll sleep soon, I imagine."

"What if I get up and go out and tell everybody?"

"No," Dr. Morton said. "I'm afraid I can't permit that. Besides, what is it you'd tell everybody, as you put it?" The doctor reached into his jacket pocket and took out a small leather case.

"I could tell about a murder," Guttman said.

"Mr. Cohen?"

"No. Miss Walters," Guttman said quietly. "And what if they decided to—what's the word?—get the body and examine it . . ."

"An exhumation." He opened the case and removed a hypodermic needle.

170

"What's that for?"

"I'm afraid your cold is going to get worse rather suddenly."

"Because of that thing?"

"Partly. Of course, your leaving the window open all night after taking a hot bath, that wasn't very clever of you in your condition."

"I didn't take a bath."

"I'll fill the tub and then empty it," Dr. Morton said. "And open the window, of course. Pneumonia is really quite serious, you know. I warned you about it."

"It's gonna look suspicious," Guttman said.

"Not at all. Old people die every day, you know."

"And what you got in the needle is gonna give me pneumonia so I get sick and die?"

"I'm afraid so, Mr. Guttman. You seem to know too much."

"What is it that I know?" Guttman asked.

"Ah, well, why don't you tell me? I'm curious to find out just how much you've learned. Before you go."

"You keep talking about me being old," Guttman said. "You're not exactly a kid, yourself."

"I'm fifty-eight," the doctor admitted.

"You look a little younger."

"Thank you."

"But fifty-eight, that would be about right. Let's see, you went to medical school, where was it?"

"Yes, Mr. Guttman. I can see you're on to it, aren't you?" The doctor looked around. "You don't have a tape recorder around here, do you?"

"If I did, you would've said too much already. But no, there's no tape recorder."

"I'll have to look later. To answer your question, Mr. Guttman, I went to medical school in New Orleans."

"It's funny, isn't it," Guttman said, "how you and Mr. Cohen happened to know each other from back then?"

"Oh?"

"Uh huh. Somebody told me about it," Guttman explained, remembering his conversation with the Bowseniors.

"Well, life is full of coincidences."

"Would you mind telling me what made you decide to come here tonight?" Guttman asked.

"A last request?" Dr. Morton asked, smiling a bit. "Very well. When I realized that Miss Brady was looking through the files, I knew that I had to keep an eye on you. And then, the other day when you mentioned the insurance, and I knew that there was nothing in the files about it, well . . ."

"You got it signed over to yourself," Guttman said. "You killed Miss Walters and worked it out so the insurance was all coming to you."

"Not at all. I see you really didn't know, did you? All of this, just a gambit to get me to come out into the open, is that it?"

"I'm here because I got a cold and my daughter wouldn't let me stay in the house alone," Guttman answered. "But it seemed like a good chance to get two birds with one stone."

"I'm afraid you miscalculated, Mr. Guttman." Dr. Morton held the hypodermic up to the light and pressed the end so a drop of liquid formed on the end of the needle.

"What was it with the insurance?" Guttman asked, edging his feet over so he'd be able to get up quickly.

"I sold it to Cohen, believe it or not. And no, I'm not trying to collect on it. It's no good, you see. Phony. I sold it to him because I needed the money to stay in school. Sold quite a few policies, as a matter of fact. Very lucrative while it lasted. I'd collect a big down payment, very large, and explain that if the purchaser lived to the age of sixty, they'd be able to collect the full amount without making any further payments."

"And you came here, and Cohen recognized you."

"Unfortunately. Of course, I didn't know who the hell he was until he started talking about New Orleans."

"How come he didn't tell anybody else about the insurance?"

"I asked him not to. That's all. Said the board wouldn't approve, something like that. And everything was fine as long as he stayed alive. Even if he'd died, there would have been no problem. Except he signed the insurance over to Miss Walters, and she was going to try to collect."

"Did she know you sold it to Cohen?"

"That's why she's dead," Morton said evenly. "And now it's your turn."

"Couldn't you have just given Cohen the money back?"

"You're marvelous, Mr. Guttman," Dr. Morton said, laughing. "Of course I could have given him the money back. But then I'd have had to admit I was party to a fraud. And how long do you think I'd have stayed on here if that happened? I'm fifty-eight. Where am I going to find another setup like this? Oh, no, Mr. Guttman. I'm not about to let this slip through my hands."

"So now I'm supposed to just sit here and let you put a needle in me?" Guttman asked.

Dr. Morton took a step closer to the bed, the needle held out in front of him. "I'm afraid this is it, Mr. Guttman."

"You ain't afraid," Guttman said. "You ain't worrying about me, and you ain't feeling sorry, so stop pretending."

Dr. Morton didn't answer, but he took another step toward Guttman.

"It's a mistake," Guttman said, raising the cane and holding it in front of him like a sword.

"I wasn't expecting that," Dr. Morton said. He backed away until he reached the dresser. Then he put the hypodermic down and turned to face Guttman again. Quickly Guttman swung his legs over the side of the bed and got to his feet. Still, the doctor's lunge took him by surprise.

Guttman managed to keep his grip on the cane, pulling back, even as Dr. Morton tried to wrench it from him. Guttman slowly began to raise the cane so that it was over their heads, and then, hips pressed back against the bed giving him a bit of support, he began using the leverage of his greater height to force the cane down. Strength I got, Guttman told himself, and I'm taller. But for how long . . . ?

"You could have a heart attack, old man . . ."

"And you could have a broken head," Guttman answered, slowly forcing the doctor to give ground. He's not so young, either, Guttman reminded himself. Fifty-eight isn't a kid . . .

The doctor leaned back, suddenly pulling Guttman forward

and twisting his two-hand grip on the cane at the same time. For an instant Guttman's grip loosened, but he managed to shove himself forward, so that when they fell, Morton took Guttman's full weight. The old man pulled back, finally getting to his feet, the cane in his hands. He raised it, and Morton lifted himself to a sitting position.

"You make a move," Guttman said, panting heavily, "and I'll hit you right on the head with this." He gasped, wanting only to sit down and catch his breath. If he'd been in front of the door when it slammed open, he would have been knocked down.

It was like a sudden invasion. He and Morton had struggled silently, and now the room was full of them, pushing one another aside in their haste to get in, each of them armed, somehow. Mishkin was first, a huge wrench in his hand, and behind him Miss Brady carrying a table lamp. Mrs. O'Rourke was behind her, waving an umbrella, and to Guttman's complete surprise, Dora Kaplan was right on Mrs. O'Rourke's heels, her arm drawn back ready to swing an oversized pocketbook. He blinked, and realized that there was still one more. Mr. Carstairs had stationed himself at the door, holding a chair up in front of him.

"Are you all right?" Miss Brady asked.

"I'm a little out of breath," Guttman mumbled, sitting down heavily.

"We heard everything," Dora Kaplan said.

"It was Miss Brady's idea," Mishkin said, standing over Dr. Morton with the wrench in his hand.

"I don't understand," Guttman said.

"We thought it best not to tell you about it," Mrs. Kaplan said. "Since you had a secret, we decided to have one, too."

"What the hell is this?" Dr. Morton asked weakly.

"This is the Golden Valley Irregulars," Margaret Brady told him. "And I think it's time someone got the police."

"I'll go," Carstairs said from the doorway.

"Everybody's here," Guttman said, still feeling stunned.

"Naturally," Mrs. Kaplan said.

"I'm sorry it took so long," Mishkin said. "The thing is, we forgot to bring anything to use. I had to go back to my room to get this," he added, holding up the wrench.

"How could you . . . I mean, I don't understand," Guttman said, noticing that his breathing was a bit more normal.

"Well, it was obvious you were setting a trap and using yourself as bait. So we just snuck into the empty room next door and listened," Miss Brady explained.

"How could you hear anything? I thought the walls was soundproof."

"Miss Brady borrowed some stethoscopes," Mrs. O'Rourke said, holding one up.

"It's amazing how well you can hear with one," Mrs. Kaplan said.

"I'm sure," Guttman said, shaking his head. He was glad for the help, and wished that he'd known about it all along. Well, he hadn't been fair with them, so why should they have told him? But, he remembered, when they arrived he'd been standing up with the weighted cane, and Dr. Morton had been on the floor. The cavalry had arrived just a little bit late. The battle was over. Still, it's nice to have a witness, Guttman thought. Better still, five witnesses.

The Golden Valley Senior Citizens' Center had never seen so much excitement. The police arrived quickly, but not before, it seemed, every resident at the Center, all asking what had happened and why they hadn't been invited. It was nearly morning before there was quiet again. But almost at dawn the excitement erupted again. The police returned to ask their questions again, and Guttman had to make a great effort not to look at Detective Weiss and say "Not everybody what's old is crazy." Reporters arrived, even television cameras, and the residents didn't know whether to back off and watch, or to get in front of the cameras to talk. The television cameras bothered Guttman most of all, though. What if Lois was watching in San Francisco? If she saw this, she'd come right back. Unfortunately, she did.

In the days that followed, the interviews and the uproar slowly died down, and Guttman found that Lois not only accepted the fact that her father was a celebrity, she enjoyed it. And, of course, he was a hero to his grandchildren, which Guttman enjoyed most of all.

Two weeks after THE night, as they called it, Miss Brady announced that Dr. Aiken, her old friend, was returning to run the Center. He was tired of being retired. All of the residents who'd known him were almost as pleased as Miss Brady. But there were disappointments, too. Mrs. Kaplan and Mrs. O'Rourke were terribly upset when they were told that Dr.

Morton had signed a confession, and would, as they said, "cop a plea," making it unnecessary for them to appear on the witness stand. Mrs. Kaplan had even bought a new dress for the occasion.

A few days before the return of Dr. Aiken, Guttman and Miss Brady were playing chess in the library while Mr. Carstairs watched, coaching whichever one of them seemed in the poorer position. Most of the time it was Guttman.

"Thinking back," Mr. Carstairs said at one point, "there's one small thing regarding our little adventure which I still don't understand. I think you worked everything out admirably, but when Dr. Morton came into your room, he thought you'd be sleeping because of the sedative you'd taken. But you were able to stay awake."

"I didn't swallow the pills," Guttman explained. "As soon as the nurse went out, I spit them out in the toilet."

"Ah," Mr. Carstairs said.

"It wouldn't have made any difference," Miss Brady said.

"Two sleeping pills wouldn't've mattered?"

"They were aspirin capsules," Miss Brady told him, smiling. "I didn't think they'd do you any harm. That was a nasty cold you had."

"You . . ." Guttman stammered. "But . . ."

"I switched the medication. Of course, the nurse didn't know about it," she added.

"But how did you know to do that?" Carstairs asked, since Guttman was simply staring with his mouth open a bit.

"Oh, I suspected Dr. Morton all along. Never did like him, you know. The only thing was, I couldn't figure out a motive for him, let alone prove it. But I knew he did it all along. If you'd asked me, I would have told you," she added, smiling at Guttman.

Guttman looked at her for a long moment, then nodded his head and smiled back at her. "Okay," he said. "So next time I'll make sure I ask right away."

About the Author

ARTHUR D. GOLDSTEIN was born in Brooklyn, attended Stuyvesant High School and Ohio University, and now lives in New York. He is currently the editor of a Wall Street publication.